ISAAC'S WILL

KRIS DURSO

Contact Information:
kdurso@yahoo.com
kdogreview.com

Design by Lili Schwartz
liliandben.com

To order additional copies, please contact the author or BookSurge.
BookSurge
www.booksurge.com
1-866-308-6235
orders@booksurge.com

CONTENTS

For my girls —
Amy, Emma, and Maggie

CHAPTER 1

MOVING

T he bare and lifeless trees whirred past Will Karras as he stared out the window of his mom's sturdy Volvo station wagon. The scenery was like his life in recent months: a blur. Before that time he was a normal and happy 15 year-old, raised in a suburban landscape by two seemingly normal and loving parents. But, like the last mile marker he saw, all that was behind him now.

It had been four months since his father, Dr. Michael Karras, dropped a bombshell on the family, announcing that he had been having an affair with a patient at his office, and that he would be leaving the family so he didn't have to "sneak around living a lie anymore." It really did come out of nowhere. No one in his family nor the tight-knit community he'd lived in his whole life saw it coming. And certainly no one expected to learn that just three months after moving out, he would lie dead in his girlfriend's apartment from a self-inflicted gunshot wound to the head.

But it happened, and a day after Will and his mother buried him, she announced that she had taken a new job an hour from their suburban Rochester hometown in the small village of Seneca Falls. They would be moving there in less than a month.

Will's bright blue eyes, his most striking feature, bounced off the passenger-side window and reflected back on him as he thought about the past months' events. He had said goodbye to everything and everyone he knew, and it dawned on him that he hadn't even begun thinking about what lie ahead.

He shifted his gaze toward his mother and a pang of guilt shot through his skinny frame as he stared at her. She looked older. Her eyes were tired and heavy, and the skin on her face seemed to sag a little bit more with the weight of each passing day.

But it wasn't just her looks that had changed. She was smoking again, something she hadn't done since her college days, and her nightly glass of wine with dinner, the norm before his father left, had been replaced with airline-sized bottles of vodka at all hours of the day. She was taking pills, too, that the doctor had prescribed to take the edge off her nerves. They dulled everything she once was, everything that Will loved and admired about her. It had all taken a huge toll on her and was slowly turning her into a stranger to her own son.

His vibrating cell phone snapped him back from under his thoughts. It was a text message from his best friend, Ian.

R u there yet?

Will smiled at the thought of him. Before Ian and his family moved to Fairport from a military base in Germany, Will spent most of his free time in a happy solitude. He had always had a small group of friends at school, but with the exception of the occasional weekend movie, rarely hung out with anyone outside of school. For the most part he was content being what Dr. Karras called him: a loner. The charismatic and outgoing chiropractor couldn't understand how a teenager could happily retreat to his room to listen to music, read, or occasionally surf the internet – alone. Will knew that in reality his father resented him. He knew Dr. Karras got embarrassed when one of his patients would ask why Will wasn't trying out for the baseball team or going to the dance on Friday night. His father wanted him to have more friends, to be more popular, to play sports, to be more like he was at Will's age. He had a hard time just accepting his son for who he was.

Within a week of Ian moving to Fairport, the two had become fast friends. They clicked with each other because neither wanted to fit into a clique. The longhaired stranger from Germany exposed Will to new music, books, and websites. Will had finally found someone who found the humor in all the insignificant seriousness of the world around him.

Following his father's suicide, the pity, and worse yet, morbid curiosity of friends and teachers at school brought the two closer together. One day he overheard his notoriously nosey computer teacher gossiping with another teacher. "I heard that his wife had a nervous breakdown," she said. Later that day she wrapped her arm around him in a phony gesture of compassion and asked how his mom was doing. Will knew that anything he said would make the lunchtime news in the teacher's lounge. *What kind of a question is that?* he thought. *Her husband left her and shot himself in the head.* He gently eased himself out from under her hug. "She's doing great," he said apathetically.

But Ian was the one person Will could trust with his thoughts and feelings. His best friend tried to optimistically convince him that it would be good to get away from Fairport, to get a fresh start. Will knew he was right, but wished he could take Ian with him.

He deftly typed his sarcastic response into the phone.

Almost there... can see the mist from the falls.

When Ian found out where Will was moving, a quick Google search told him that there were no waterfalls in Seneca Falls. He sadly broke the news to Will.

"Who are you texting?" his mother asked.

"Ian."

"It'll do you good to get away from him. You shouldn't spend so much time with one person." Her hands shook as she pulled a cigarette from a pack on the dashboard. "He'll probably just forget about you anyway."

Will ignored the comment and turned to look back out the window. The mud-snow mix sloshed under the tires while the dreary scenery raced past him. He closed his eyes and drifted off into sleep, afraid to wake up to the next chapter of his life.

CHAPTER 2

SENECA FALLS

T he tall green water tower with *Seneca Falls* written in fancy script letters greeted Will when he opened his eyes. The letters were a stark contrast to the landscape below. Directly across the street was a battered "Starlite Motel" sign fronting a burned-out group of low-end single-story motel rooms. It must have been a bad fire, he thought. In fact, it was a bad fire, set by a well-connected local boy two years ago. Everyone in the small village knew who masterminded the blaze, and everyone also knew that he would be left unpunished. The Baker family was untouchable.

There was talk of rebuilding, but since the knitting mill and Sylvania television plant closed down there were more people leaving the town than visiting. Tourists did come to visit the National Women's Hall of Fame, but opted for the nicer hotels in Rochester or Syracuse over the run-down motels of Seneca Falls. And this was really a shame. Snugly nestled in the heart of the Finger Lakes, the village was surrounded by natural beauty. But like the lakes that were carved out by glaciers millions of years ago, Seneca Falls was slowly being worn down by layoffs and economic despair. In spite of the bottomless lakes, the town was drying up.

His mother had accepted a job at one of the only remaining lifelines of the town, the New York State Chiropractic College, a business she knew well considering that she spent years helping her husband run his office. She had worked there since they were married some twenty years ago, warmly greeting patients, helping with x-rays, and minding the books and appointments.

Past the motel was an ice cream shop closed for the long and dark winter, and farther down the road a weather-battered bar sat with a parking lot filled with Sunday drinkers waiting for the Bills game to start.

But as his mother neared a fork in the road heading toward the downtown business district, the scenery changed. Century-old oak and maple trees appeared from the barren landscape, framing huge brick houses from another era. Their well-manicured lawns led the way to tall and impressive columns on the homes' front porches. Will admired a cupola perched atop a three story historical mansion.

"Is this where we'll be living?" he asked hopefully.

His mother rolled her eyes, hissing like she had sprung a leak. "No. This is Cayuga Street. Our house is on the *other* side of the canal."

He wasn't surprised by her cold reaction. His father's death took a much bigger toll on her than it did on him.

The warm tones coming from her inviting face that he had grown to expect over the past fourteen years were replaced with sarcastic snaps and bitter sneers. Will was learning to accept it as a product of the separation and suicide. Could he blame her?

Cayuga Street continued past more glorious trees and houses, across the train tracks that ran through the front yard of the three-story brick high school he'd be starting at tomorrow, and finally intersected with Fall Street, the main drag of the village. His mother feathered the brakes and they came to rest at a stoplight. Vacant stores hid behind dusty glass storefronts like empty shells from a distant time. Some of their signs still survived, headstones for the dead pharmacies, restaurants, and hardware stores lining the street.

Will watched as a group of teenagers huddled together smoking cigarettes on a bench in front of a bar with *Filthy McNasty's* etched in faded yellow letters on its window. One of them, a heavy-set blonde-haired boy caught his gaze. Will felt the stranger's deep-set eyes burning into him. The boy said something to the others and they all turned to stare at him. It wasn't the welcome he was hoping for. The light finally turned green, and even after the strangers were out of sight, Will could still feel their eyes penetrating through the back window.

They crossed the short bridge over the Barge Canal, now drained for winter maintenance, and the deep and empty chasm reminded him of the downtown he had just passed. Once over the bridge they turned left and into a shrubless landscape littered with the remains of a deserted ruler factory, a run-down IGA grocery store, and small houses crammed together. This was the street they'd be living on – Bayard Street – and if Will wasn't excited about the scenery on the way to his house, he certainly had no way to prepare himself for his new home – or more importantly – what lie behind it.

CHAPTER 3

RESTVALE

With its left turn signal blinking, the car slowed and his mother carefully pointed it up a short and steep concrete ramp that led to a gravel driveway. The Volvo scraped its front end, letting out a sickly growl. A worn brick facade with a plaque reading "Restvale" greeted them. It was a cemetery.

"Why are we stopping here?"

His mother sighed and blew a string of gray-streaked hair out of her eyes. "We're stopping here because this is where we'll be living."

"We're living in a graveyard," Will said flatly in disbelief.

She mashed her cigarette out in the ashtray. "Will, we're not living in a graveyard. The house is on the cemetery grounds. It used to be the caretaker's house, and it's all we can afford right now."

They stopped at the bottom of a hill about a hundred yards from the cemetery entrance. A dilapidated two-story dwelling with faded and flaking paint sat before them. A deep gully littered with thick briar patches, its steep walls climbing to the cemetery above, provided an eerie background. This was their new home.

Two rotting wicker rocking chairs covered with three inches of snow rested on the front porch. Will followed his mother out of the car and gazed up at the small round cupola crookedly sitting atop the weather-beaten shingles. The sound of their steps sent a squirrel scurrying from under the porch as they stepped over a missing plank and opened the door.

The inside of the house wasn't any nicer than the outside. In fact, no one had lived there in more than ten years. A thick layer of dust covered the wood living room floor and black and white checked linoleum in the kitchen. The gaudy green appliances looked like a page from a 1975 Sears catalog. A stairway directly facing the side door led the way upstairs to what would become Will's bedroom. His mother would take the only other bedroom downstairs.

Will knew why they had to live in such a place, but that didn't make it any easier. The only home he had known his whole life was a two-story split-level in an upscale neighborhood in suburban Rochester. He knew that his father had squandered most of the money he'd made in his 20-year practice in the months leading up to his suicide. In that time he racked up tens of thousands of dollars in credit card debt that his mother was now responsible for paying. She sold the practice only to learn that he had stopped making rental payments on the property and owed thousands more in back rent. To top it all off, he sold his life insurance to pay for the luxuries of his new life. These included: breast implants for his girlfriend, a two-week trip to Hawaii, and a week of gambling in Las Vegas (he lost $10,000 in just one night at the blackjack table).

Will set his book bag, his only possession until the moving truck arrived, down at the top of the stairs. He could see his small, dank bedroom directly to the right, and decided he didn't want to see anymore.

"I'm going for a walk," he yelled, running down the stairs.

"Don't be gone too long. I'm going to need your help getting this place straightened up."

He couldn't believe that he was here, living in a house in front of a graveyard with headstones stretching out as far as he could see. So much had changed in a year, he thought, as he continued further into the depths of the cemetery. This time last year he lived in a neighborhood filled with the sights and sounds of people blowing snow, mowing grass, walking, talking, and playing with their kids. Everything here was lifeless; silent.

He dodged a pothole and thought about his father. They were never close because of the long hours he kept at the office. Dr. Karras was one of the few chiropractors in Rochester whose office was open until 9pm, four nights a week. That was how and when he met Debbie, his girlfriend.

Will snapped from his memories, taking in the scenery around him. The gravel drive ran parallel to Bayard Street for a short distance before turning left and heading deep into the oldest part of the cemetery. There it looped back around and rejoined the main drive at the front of the graveyard.

The names on the headstones looked Italian and were unfamiliar to him. Most ended in vowels - Battaglia, Baldassari, Cappaci – names from generations of families that had settled in the small town when it was a fruitful village in the early 20th century. Most of Fairport and his own family were of Greek descent. His friends constantly made jokes about his mom and the milkman since he was the only Greek in town with blonde hair and blue eyes.

Will watched the trees mimic the sky: big, bare, and gray. They were mostly oaks, some with huge knots growing from their sides, and had to be, he thought, at least a hundred years old. They framed the driveway at odd intervals, their confused and crooked limbs stretching out over him.

He tried to repress any memories he'd had of his father's death, but they were always there at the back of his mind, desperately calling for attention, and quietly creeping into his consciousness. The setting brought them forward now, and he decided not to fight them. There was no point in it considering this was the first time he'd been near, let alone *in* a cemetery since he and his mother buried his father. He let his father's picture, his dark black hair and eyes, develop in his mind. The memories of the good times would come back to him later in his life, but for now the morbid thoughts raced and swirled around in his head.

Everything he knew about that fateful night came from police reports created from interviews with Debbie. Michael

Karras, it said, died on a Friday night of a self-inflicted gunshot wound to the head. He had been more irritable than usual, his easy-going demeanor taking a back seat to strange behavior in the nights leading up to the suicide. Debbie awoke several times that week to find Michael out of bed, sitting alone in the dark slowly swaying back and forth in a rocking chair in her living room.

Will imagined him staring blankly into the nothingness of the night, just as Debbie had described to the police, not responding to her words, just rocking and staring. She gently tried to snap him out of it, but couldn't break the invisible barrier between himself and his own mind. Deeply disturbed, she returned to the bedroom where she would wake alone, only to find him the next morning slumped in the rocking chair asleep.

But when Friday came, Debbie told the police, his mood had changed. He was happy and carefree, his whole demeanor doing a complete 180. He had slept well Thursday night, making it through the whole night in their bed. His mood was still soaring after work that day. He was excited that they were going out to dinner with some of his old friends. He showered first, joking about a favorite patient he had seen earlier that day, and began to get dressed as Debbie hopped into the shower. She gave him a playful yell when she got out.

"Michael?"

No answer.

"Michael? Hey, do you want me to wear the black dress you like so much?" she called.

Nothing.

"Michael. Are you all right? Hello," she sang walking down the hall to the living room with a towel draped around her.

The room was dark and all the lights were out. Her heart dropped as she heard the familiar sound of the creaking rocking chair rhythmically swaying. He sat in his boxers and t-shirt, staring into the dark, a nine-millimeter pistol resting on his lap. A streetlight provided enough light for her to make out his figure in the chair, and, as her eyes adjusted, the blank and emotionless look painted on his face.

"What are you doing? We're going to be la..."

"It's no good." His voice was already dead.

She watched him lift the gun to his mouth, his lips twisting into a maniacal smile. The look splashed across his entire face the moment before he pulled the trigger. The flash lit the room, and it was over.

The loud cackle of a black crow sitting on a nearby six-foot pointed monument snapped Will from the memory. He realized he had been walking for quite some time on autopilot, unaware of his own movements let alone his surroundings. He had made it to the far end of the cemetery, about three football fields from Bayard Street. The potholed road narrowed to a muddy path.

This part of Restvale was split into three sections separated by the poorly manicured road. He walked to his left, toward a tree line, dodging weather-beaten monuments from the early 1800's. This was the "old" part of the cemetery, and the grave markers showed it not only with the dates but with the names as well - Vincenzo, Mary, Antoinette, Salvatore, Wilhelmus - were a few that caught his eye.

He made it to the trees and leaned against part of a black wrought iron fence. The trees struggled to balance themselves against a steep slope that led down 100 feet to the still and muddy-green waters of the canal. He looked across the canal to a rusty water tower with *Sylvania* scrawled across it in faded paint.

As he stared at the gloomy landscape, a moving shadow caught the corner of his eye off to his left. He turned his head toward it, and in the fleeting minutes of daylight that remained, made out what appeared to be an old man, tall and thin and donning a fedora hat, walking toward him.

A wailing car horn drew Will's attention away from the shadow. He jumped and turned his head to the right. It was his mom.

Will turned and walked toward her car, squinting in the fading light to find the stranger whom he had just seen. But no one was there.

CHAPTER 4

MYNDERSE

ilhelmus Mynderse's tall and faded bronze statue stood in front of the school that bore his name. It was the first thing Will saw as his mother drove toward the student drop-off. The only other time he went to a new school was when he started kindergarten at Frank Knight Elementary in Fairport when he was five. He wondered if he was as nervous then as he was today as faded movies of his father dropping him off played through his mind.

"Have a good day," she said unenthusiastically between drags of her cigarette.

"Yeah, sure," he responded without emotion. He closed the car door and headed toward the front entrance.

The February morning was cold and dark, and he was virtually unnoticed by the other students that rushed to the doors with their heads down waiting for the relief of the heat inside. But once inside, their eyes descended upon him in curiosity. Lifelong friends talked in hushed, morning-dazed tones about, he assumed, the "new kid."

He stood, alone, waiting for the homeroom bell, awkwardly shifting his weight from one foot to the other, trying not to appear exactly what he was: scared. He remembered seeing other kids on their first day at a new school, wondering what they must be thinking.

When the bell finally rang, he followed the crowd as they slowly pushed through the scarred wooden doors, each on a mission to get to their lockers and then to homeroom. He kept his head down, staying close to the wall looking only at the feet in front of him. Occasionally he glanced up to see if he could spot the front office. A trophy case filled with the relics of past pennants, trophies, and photos of bygone championships jutted out from the wall ahead of him, revealing the office just past it.

Will stepped through the glass doors. The passing students outside were drowned out by the sounds of typing fingers, soft conversation, and the mellow sounds of 70's rock gently pushing the air through the speakers of a small boom box.

"Can I help you?" a middle-aged woman asked, looking over her glasses as she finished typing.

"I'm Will Karras," he said quietly. "I'm new here."

"You need to go to the guidance counselor to get your schedule," she said smiling. "And welcome to Mynderse Academy!" she added enthusiastically.

He turned to go, but realized he didn't know where or whom the guidance counselor was.

"Uh, where's her office?"

"Miss Brick's office? Go out the door, take a right down the hall, and it's the last door on the left," she said smiling.

"Thanks," he said, forcing a smile.

Will made his way down the hall, his eyes still fixed to the floor. An occasional glance revealed boys leaning against their lockers, trying to look cool for their girlfriends, who had their books against their chests, leaning into the conversation. He could feel their eyes upon him, watching his every move, whispering about the "new kid." He was back at Fairport High again, he thought, reliving his first day back after his father's funeral.

He navigated against traffic to Miss Brick's office and opened the heavy, frosted Plexiglas door. The "u" and "i" were scratched out on the word "Guidance," cleverly replaced in black *Sharpie* with an "a" and "y." The office was cluttered with files and papers scattered across ancient wooden desks marred with decades of graffiti. There was a map with push pins showing where this year's seniors would be attending college, mostly in New York State, and a few randomly placed character trait posters featuring multi-racial students acting out things like "Respect" and "Responsibility."

Miss Brick was on the telephone, and smilingly motioned Will to sit in a vinyl cushioned green chair in front of her desk. She was younger than the counselor at his old school, with short blonde hair and a trusting face. Will's eyes panned quickly across her desk, only registering the colors of yellow *Post It* notes, red and black pens, and then...blue. His pupils darted back to a photograph of Miss Brick with a man with blonde hair and striking blue eyes, both dressed up with their arms around each other.

She hung up the phone.

"Will?" she questioned, eyebrows raised and smiling.

He didn't hear her, his eyes still planted firmly on the photograph.

"Wiiiilllllll..." she sang, trying to break the trance.

He heard her this time and shook his head to erase the image from his mind. Will lifted his gaze toward her and couldn't help returning the warm smile. "Yeah," he said.

"Welcome!" she said, and from what Will could tell she actually meant it. Relief swept over his face for the first time since moving to Seneca Falls.

She asked about where he was from, where he was living (if she was shocked that he lived in a cemetery she didn't show it), where his mom was working, and if he had met anyone in town yet. She knew about his father, and without coming right out and saying it, made it clear that he was always welcome in her office if he needed anything. He believed her.

"This is your schedule," she said, handing him a half-sheet of paper with dot matrix printer writing on it. "I asked one of our freshmen, Robert, to kind of get you acquainted with the school. He's in almost all of your classes. I thought it'd be good to have someone show you around a little bit."

"Thanks," Will said, his eyes moving from hers to the floor.

She picked up the phone again and dialed a few

numbers. "Hey, it's Angela. Could you send Robert down to my office? Thanks," she giggled into the mouthpiece and hung up. "He'll be right down."

A minute later the door opened, and Robert walked in. The boys exchanged "Heys," Robert offering his hand for a shake.

It wasn't an accident that Miss Brick chose Robert to be Will's "buddy." He was a good student, was responsible and trustworthy, and most importantly had overcome some monumental challenges in his own life. His parents had recently split up, and his father was serving a twelve-year sentence at Attica State Penitentiary.

Succumbing to the pressures, Robert fell into a deep depression of his own as he helplessly watched his whole world crumble around him. Unable to cope with the realities of life, he began hanging out with the "wrong" crowd, and started smoking pot daily – before, during, and after school. Initially the drugs did a good job of dulling the pain, but as his tolerance built up, he found himself having to smoke more and more just to get high. When two of his "friends" tried to convince him to steal money from his mother's purse, he decided he had had enough. Without any outside intervention, he just stopped, realizing that he was headed for the same fate as his father.

He started hanging out with a different group of kids. They weren't as popular, but he didn't care. Although he wasn't an all-star student at the top of his class, Robert traded in his D's and F's for B's and the occasional A.

His confidence rose, and for the first time in a long time he was happy with his life. Anyone who knew what he had been through and how he had eventually come out – through his own determination – understood why he carried himself with a confidence not usually found in a ninth grader.

As the two were getting ready to leave Miss Brick's office, Robert snapped his fingers and pointed at Will. He flipped quickly on his heels and faced the counselor. "I couldn't figure it out at first, but I kept thinking he looked like someone I knew." He paused waiting for Miss Brick to solve his mystery. She raised her eyebrows, expectantly waiting for the answer.

"Larsen," he announced. "He kinda looks like Larsen."

Miss Brick shifted her eyes from Robert to Will, her smile replaced with a curious acknowledgement. She nodded, still studying Will's face.

Robert turned to Will. "You look like her boyfriend, Larsen. The guy in that picture," he said pointing at the photo on the desk.

"He's not my boyfriend," she objected, blushing. "He's just a good friend." There was no use in trying to convince Robert or the rest of the school that the two weren't a couple. Everyone knew it to be true, even though in reality it wasn't.

Robert looked at Will and smiled. "Right. I meant to say that they were just friends...very *very* good friends."

Miss Brick shook her head. "Go!" she said to Robert,

playfully pointing at the door.

"Tell your special friend I said 'Hi'," Robert jabbed, and led Will out to the hall and into his first day at Mynderse.

With the door shut behind them, Miss Brick stared at Larsen's photo. Robert was right about one thing, she thought: Will did sort of look like him.

CHAPTER 5

HISTORY REPEATS ITSELF

R obert said something to Will, but the crowd of people drowned out his words.

"What?" Will asked.

"Forget it," Robert yelled, "We'll talk when we get to homeroom."

Navigating their way down the halls, Will saw faces he recognized from his old school. They obviously weren't the same kids he had left back in Fairport, but they were all familiar to him. There were jocks puffing their chests out of their oversized basketball jerseys, burnouts with red eyes giggling at nothing in particular, pre-pubescents spazzing and doing something stupid for any attention to cover up the fact that they had made it to high school before they fully developed, freaks with piercings and over-dyed hair, and nerds with books stuffed under their skinny or fat arms, staring straight ahead, comfortable only in their own bedrooms – and barely even there. He knew them all, and if he had moved here before his father left and killed himself it would have given him some sense of comfort. But the sight of them only made his heart race and his hands sweat.

They finally made it to homeroom, and before they even walked through the door, a flamboyantly dressed middle-aged man greeted them. It was Mr. Galero, the History teacher. "Helllllooooo!" he belted out excitedly. "You must be our new student." Will smiled and followed Robert to the back of the room to an empty chair, hoping to somehow make himself invisible.

For the most part he was. The groggy and bleary-eyed teenagers whose bodies beg to be out of a fluorescent-lit classroom and back in the warmth and comfort of their own bed barely noticed him until Mr. Galero announced a new name during morning roll call. Heads pivoted on strained necks to get a look at the new kid at the back of the room. The girls wanted to see if he was "hot," something fresh to look at in a school that had seen more people move out than in, while most of the boys just glanced and turned back around. Not wanting to disturb their morning buzz, two of the burnouts didn't even bother to lift their heads off their desks.

One boy, however, snapped his head back violently at the mention of Will's name. He stared, trying to force the corners of his mouth down from the twisted grin that crept over his face.

Will absorbed the stranger's curiosity, and then recognized him as the same heavy-set blonde haired boy who coldly stared at him when he and his mother first drove into town. The two were locked onto each other for only a second before he averted his eyes to the fresh schedule on his desk. But in that second, he sensed that this boy, whoever he was, already knew him.

His name was Stanton Baker. His father, Douglas, was the Dean of Student Affairs at the Finger Lakes Chiropractic College, and more importantly, Will's mother's boss. Stanton, like his father, was not liked by the majority of people in the village, but also like his father, held some sort of power over them. He was a highly intelligent kid who used his brains to manipulate situations around him, stirring the pot, and then sitting back to watch the mess boil over for his own amusement. Earlier in the year he hacked into the school's computer, pretending to be a senior who had threatened to beat him up for talking trash about his girlfriend. Stanton sent a bomb threat from the boy's account, vividly describing the carnage he intended to bring to Mynderse Academy, its faculty, and student body. The senior was charged with a felony (later dropped to a misdemeanor), given five years probation, and expelled from school. In all that time Stanton never felt a moment of remorse, and actually took great pride in ruining the senior's life.

Physically he was short and stubby and wore baggy t-shirts and flannels to cover his flab. It was hard to believe that he was a third-degree black belt in judo, but he was. Always ready and willing to use his weight as leverage to throw kids around or grab certain pressure points on their wrists to bring them to submission, all out of the sight of teachers and adults, Stanton Baker was an enigma.

His pure evil was legendary in the town. One day he caught up to a seventh grader walking home alone from school, and asked him if he wanted to learn a Judo move. The seventh grader, knowing Stanton's reputation, said no and kept his eyes focused on his feet. Stanton stepped in front of him, blocking his way.

"I asked you if you wanted to learn a Judo move," he demanded.

The boy tried to walk around him, and as he did, Stanton extended both arms at an angle out in front of him and viciously clapped the boy's ears with his hands. The boy fell to the ground, dizzy, having suffered two popped eardrums. His parents tried to press charges against Stanton, but he denied ever seeing the boy, and with no witnesses, nothing ever came of it.

Such was the power he had over his classmates. Most, even the biggest kids in the class, were afraid of him and kept their distance. Realizing he was a better ally than enemy, a small group of "friends" sheepishly followed his every direction.

Will watched Stanton tap a boy sitting next to him on the shoulder and point back toward him. The boy eagerly turned around and motioned another student sitting a few rows back. Stanton, now with an audience, tilted his head to one side, pursed his lips, and raised his eyebrows in a mocking "I feel so sorry for you," expression. After a quick glance to be sure Mr. Galero wasn't looking, he extended his pointer finger and thumb into the shape of a gun, turned the mock pistol to his head, dropped the thumb-hammer and mouthed the word, "Bang!"

Robert saw everything. Stanton, the predator, smiled broadly as he watched his prey's face turn pale, the blood rushing from his cheeks. Will slumped in his chair, defeated and seemingly dead.

The first period bell snapped time back into motion. Will managed to stand up, shaken.

"Are you okay?" Robert asked.

He didn't respond, and mechanically headed for the door. The faces in the hall were burnt shadows pulsating in and out of focus.

"Will. You don't look so good."

"Yeah," Will responded in a haze. He couldn't believe what he had just seen. No one could possibly know about his father. Could they? He couldn't imagine how he should respond, had never *had* to respond to any horror like this. No one could be that cruel.

"Come on, man," Robert encouraged him. Even at such an ominous moment, Will realized how lucky he was to have been teamed up with Robert. He had a tangible compassion not often found in a high school freshman. The boy with such an unremarkable name, Robert Jones, carried a remarkable capacity of caring and understanding.

They walked through the hall in silence and toward the cafeteria for first period Study Hall. It was a large room reeking of stale water and disinfectant. A long row of windows framed the depressing scene outside: gray skies hovering low over a gravel parking lot with two army-green dumpsters partially concealing a soccer field with torn goals and splintered bleachers. The dreary picture summed up his first hour at Mynderse.

An old woman with a beehive hairdo, surrounded mostly by jocks with basketball jerseys, sat at a table near the entrance. Robert led Will, virtually unnoticed by the other students, to a secluded table in the back of the room. A draft from the windows sent a chill through his body.

"Are you okay?" Robert asked again.

Will stared out the window. "Who was that kid in homeroom?" he asked, ignoring Robert's question.

Robert hissed. "That's Stanton Baker."

The last name rang a bell in Will's mind. Dr. Baker was his mom's boss, he remembered. "Does his dad work at the Chiropractic College?"

Robert seemed unimpressed. "Yeah. He's a dean or something down there – they're loaded, and Stanton's an idiot."

After sharing a couple of Stanton stories, Robert finally asked the question that had been on his mind since homeroom half an hour ago. "You don't have to tell me, but what was that gun thing all about in homeroom?"

Will sighed and turned to look out the window.

"I shouldn't have asked. It's none of my business," Robert apologized. "Don't worry about it, man. You can tell me whenever you feel like it or you don't have to tell me at all."

Most of the kids in the study hall were upperclassmen that Robert knew only well enough to say "Hi" to in passing, so there were no introductions to be made. The two boys sat together, Will being carefully and cautiously open with Robert, telling him bits and pieces of the whole story. His parents, he said, had had some marital problems so they moved from Fairport to Seneca Falls when his mom was offered a new job.

With nearly identical schedules, Will shadowed Robert throughout the day to English second period, Social Studies, third, French fourth, and around noon, to lunch.

Will ordered the spaghetti, paid for it, and followed Robert out into the cafeteria's dining area. Even through the noise and chaos of 100 teenagers eating lunch, he could feel the curious stares descending upon him. He walked by Stanton's table, pretending not to notice his gang smirking and pointing at him. "Is that him?" he heard one of them ask.

They finally sat down at the same table they were at during study hall. Robert sat next to a tiny blonde haired boy who looked more like a sixth grader than a high school freshman. Will sat across from Robert, next to a pock-faced boy with drooping shoulders and dull eyes.

"Hey guys," Robert started, "this is Will." He pointed to the short boy next to him. "That's Alex, and that's Travis," he added looking at the boy next to Will. Travis stood up politely to shake Will's hand while Alex looked up briefly, nodded, and pushed his thick glasses back up his nose. He was more interested in fishing out any cheesy sawdust remnants at the bottom of his *Cheez Puffs* bag. Will was facing Stanton's table, and he couldn't help himself from sneaking a quick peak to see if he was still the center of their attention. Unfortunately he was. He shifted uncomfortably in his chair hoping that his table's conversation would drown out their stares. But the boys didn't say very much to each other, leaving Will to dig at his cafeteria spaghetti wrapped up in his own thoughts.

Finally Travis spoke up. "W-w-why is S-s-s-stanton s-s-s-staring at u-u-us?" Even through his obvious speech impediment, Will detected the uncomfortable fear in his voice.

Robert turned around in his chair.

"Don't l-l-l-look at them!" Travis snapped.

He ignored him, and lifted his hand, smiling admiringly, and flitted his fingers in a dainty wave. He topped it all off by blowing a kiss to their leader.

Will watched Stanton's face turn three different shades of red as he stood up, his eyes locked on their table. "He's c-c-c-coming!" Travis gasped. Alex turned around quickly and slumped deep down in his chair. Stanton lumbered over and stood at the end of their table, coldly staring down on Robert.

He glanced toward the doors and saw the principal, Mr. Macini, surveying the room. He was a heavy-set middle-aged man with puffy cheeks and an overbite that earned him the nickname "the chipmunk."

"You're lucky that idiot rodent principal's in here," Stanton said evenly.

Robert looked up with a grin. "Stanton, man, go away. I was just playing." Will was impressed with Robert's casual tone.

"No, no, Robert, I *know* you were just playing. I

figured your dad learned that queer little wave from one of his boyfriends in prison and taught it to you." He laughed, impressed with his own joke.

Will waited for Robert's reaction, but it wasn't what he expected. He smiled, unfazed, and even let out a giggle of his own. "Ha ha ha," Robert mocked. "I expected something more clever from you, Stanton."

Stanton's eyes flashed in anger, and he shifted his attention to Will. "You're a great addition to this group. It's like Misfit Island here. You've got the s-s-s-tuttering idiot, the midget, the felon's son, and now you." He lowered his voice, addressing the other three boys. "You guys just better watch out. Your new friend here might not be around very long. I understand suicidal tendencies can run in the family. You better keep your eye on him."

Stanton lunged toward Alex in a mock attack that sent him reeling backwards and tumbling out of his seat. The noise from the sliding chair caught everyone's attention just in time to see Alex fall to the floor with a thud. The audience laughed and gave him a rousing round of applause. Stanton joined in as he headed back to his table. By the time Alex had picked himself up, Mr. Macini was drawing near their table.

"Try to keep all six feet on the floor, Alex," he said with a smile before continuing his patrol. Alex's face was beet red, and for a minute Will thought he was going to cry.

"That punk!" Robert sneered.

"Wh-wh-wh-o M-m-m-acini?" asked Travis innocently.

Robert rolled his eyes and threw his dirty napkin at him. "No, you dork. *Stanton*, not Macini."

"Did your father kill himself?" Alex asked tactlessly.

"Shut up, Alex!" Robert snapped. "Man, Stanton's right. You guys are a bunch of misfits."

The conversation died there, and Will spent the rest of the period twirling his uneaten spaghetti with his fork. Stanton's comment had flushed the color out of his face, giving it a sickly pale hue. When the bell finally rang, he followed Robert to the garbage can and threw his tray away.

Robert could tell Will was shaken. "Man, don't worry about him," he said. "I'll see you in Science last period."

Will nodded and forced a smile before heading to the gym for PE. Alex scurried to his side. "Sorry about what I said in there," he apologized sincerely.

Will found it impossible to be mad at his awkward new friend. "It's alright." He played the cafeteria chair scene over in his head and couldn't stop himself from giggling. Alex looked up at him, at first confused, then smiling knowingly.

"I know," he laughed. "It must have looked pretty funny." His nasally voice provided the perfect soundtrack for his body. Will laughed harder when he realized Alex could laugh at himself.

"We both can laugh today," he continued. "I overheard Stanton saying that he was signing out early today. I guess he won't be in PE with you today."

Will's smile flashed from his face, his eyes wide. "Stanton's in my PE class?"

"Yeah, but not today. He always picks on me, but maybe he'll give me a break now that you're here. You know, new blood for him to feed on."

"Thanks for the encouragement."

Alex smiled and pushed his glasses up. "Good luck." he said, and turned toward the computer lab.

As it turned out, Alex was right. PE, led by the stereotypical Coach Barnes, was uneventful. Will didn't have to dress out so he watched the boys play basketball from the bleachers while his mind wandered back to Fairport and his PE classes there. It's all the same, he thought: shirts and skins, the jocks pleading to be skins for the chance to show off their chiseled bodies to any girls that might pass by; the nerds just trying to stay out of the way, awkwardly running up and down the court and never daring to touch the ball; the burnouts walking, exhausted, coughing up lungs after the slightest exertion. All through the class he couldn't shake Stanton from his mind. Will realized that Stanton's father must have told him about his father's suicide which meant that everyone else in the school would know in a matter of days if they didn't already. He knew he couldn't outrun this one – not in a lifetime. He also knew that he didn't know how to handle Stanton. No one had ever bullied him like this before.

After PE he met Robert in the hall and the two walked to their uneventful Earth Science class. They both lived on the "other side of the canal," and when the final bell rang, Robert invited Will to walk home with him.

The air was cold, but the sun shined blindingly brightly off the snow, bringing the squiggly lines inside the boys' eyes to life.

"What happened in PE?" Robert asked.

"Nothing. I mean, Stanton signed out so he wasn't in there today."

"Man I'd like to beat the crap out of that kid."

"Seems like somebody would've by now."

"No. No one's even tried since like the fourth grade. He put a sixth grader in the hospital with some kind of karate move crap. Since then, no one's messed with him. A lot of people want to, but it sucks because everyone knows he could probably kill us – literally."

Will listened to the snow crunching under his feet. "You don't act like you're scared of him."

"I guess it's 'cause I'm not," Robert said casually. There was a long pause before he continued. "Will, I've had a lot of junk happen to me in my life. My dad's in prison for armed robbery. I've screwed up with drugs, my mom busts her back working two jobs, and we still live in a run-down trailer. I've dealt with all of that, and I've come out alright." He paused. "Could Stanton kill me? Yes," he said, answering his own question, "but, and I don't want to sound all dramatic, but after what I've been through, even death doesn't scare me all too much."

The words sank into Will, and neither one of them spoke for a while. His mind spun from the day's events.

"What about you?" Robert asked. "Obviously something happened to you in Fairport that made you move here." He checked himself. "I mean, you don't have to tell me what happened, but you had to have a Stanton Baker at your old school, right?"

Will ran the cast of his life's characters through his head. "No. There were people that bullied kids, but I've never met anyone like Stanton."

"Did you ever get into fights there?"

Will answered that one quickly. "No. I've only been in one fight in my whole life – and that was with Eddie Gallo in the sixth grade. We both just kind of wrestled each other to the ground and some teacher broke us apart."

They were nearing the Cayuga Street Bridge.

"What about friends? Did you have many?" Robert asked.

Will thought about Ian. "No. I mean, I didn't not have friends, but I pretty much just hung out with one kid. I guess I just never got bothered by anyone – you know, just kind of got along. Everything was good there up until..." he stopped short of telling Robert about his father, and then swerved the conversation in another direction. "You know, moving was kinda tough."

His answer was just vague enough for Robert to know not to press him any further. Instead he told Will about Justin, his best friend who had moved away to North Carolina at the end of last year. He laughed when he talked about Alex and Travis, admitting their obvious weaknesses while defending their character.

They were nearing Robert's street, their cheeks red from the cold. "I have to work tonight at Venice," Robert said. Will looked confused. "It's a pizza place on Fall Street. I'll give you a call during my break."

After a quick handshake the two left each other. Will survived his first day at school, and the cemetery lie just ahead.

CHAPTER 6

ISAAC

Ellen Karras lay passed out on the couch, still in her work clothes, when Will walked through the door. Her skirt and blouse were wrinkled, and a half-dead bottle of *Kamchatka* vodka sat on the floor next to some prescription pills. Moving boxes with black *Sharpie* writing scrawled on their sides stood at attention around the room, blocking out any light from the windows.

Trying not to wake her, Will gingerly walked by, but the creaky wooden floor gave him away. He watched her stretch out like a waking baby, her eyelids half-open. He studied her face. The move had eroded a couple of new gorges in her tired skin. Her overly done makeup gave her the appearance of a clown. Will looked away, feeling guilty about his observations.

She yawned, her voice listless. "You're home from school? Already?"

"Yeah."

It wasn't easy for him to see her like this. The mother he knew was hard working and always busy. When she wasn't working at his father's office she was helping at his school and in the community. She was a member of the PTA, and even set up a school fundraiser for a local homeless shelter that raised more than $5,000. Will remembered a time – not so long ago – when she was there for friends and neighbors in need. She was the mom other kids wished they'd had.

"It's 4:00," he said, staring at the remnants of the bottles on the floor.

She followed his gaze to the drugs, but didn't make an effort to hide it. Will watched her nonchalantly rub her eyes and stretch. Her brash behavior scared him. When her drinking problem started she would at least try to get rid of the empty bottles or cover her breath with mouth freshener.

She reached for a glass of water on an upturned cardboard box; it was their temporary version of an end table. "How was school?" Her voice was gruff and listless.

Will ignored her question. "Aren't you supposed to be at work?" he asked accusingly. The sound of his voice surprised him, and it wasn't the first time he'd noticed it. Since his dad's suicide he'd noted the tone he had been taking with her. Their roles were changing, almost reversing.

"I had a headache so I took a half day," she said. "I'll work all day tomorrow."

Will shook his head and walked upstairs to his room. He needed to get out, to get away from her. He threw down his book bag and headed back downstairs and for the door. "I'm going for a walk," he said, but there was no one there to hear him. His mother was already sprawled on the couch again, fast asleep.

The temperature was dropping as dusk approached. Darkness came early during winter in Upstate NY. Will watched the fog from his breath momentarily cloud his vision as he walked back down the gravel drive into the far recesses of the cemetery. He didn't like the cold, but the thought of being holed up in his bare room drove him deeper into it. As he walked he couldn't drive the picture of what his mother was becoming out of his mind. He tried to blur it, push it away, but it always came back to the front of his thoughts, growing sharper and more focused with each step.

He thought more about life in the past few months than he had in all his fifteen years. Why was he here? How did he get here? What was the point of it all if in the end he's only going to die? It was death that bothered him the most, and living in a graveyard wasn't helping him escape it. His thoughts sped like a cold engine: *all of these skeletons of all of these people who were once walking around just like me... they're where my father is now, and where I'll be someday... maybe sooner than later...where are they?...where is he?...my mother's turning into them...it probably won't be long until she's lying in the ground, too...*

His heart raced with his mind. Without realizing it he began to run, trying to beat his thoughts to the imaginary finish line that he and everyone fortunate enough to live would eventually have to cross. But he couldn't win. Images of his father, mother, and now Stanton bounced around in his head. *I can't win...no one can win...I can't outrun any of it...*

He stopped dead in his tracks, winded, and put his hands on his knees. His lungs burned from the cold with each breath. Unaware of his whereabouts, he looked up to find himself in the exact same spot he had ended up the first time he ventured into the cemetery: at the black iron fence overlooking the canal below.

A thin but strong voice called out. "I thought you were gonna run right off the edge."

He jumped back, startled, and brushed against someone or something. He whipped his head around and found himself staring into a man's chin, just inches away from him.

"Can't outrun life," the stranger's voice, gentle and quiet now, spoke again.

Will took another step back, frightened, and took the man in full view. He was old and tall – more than six feet – his thin frame covered by a black suit from another time. The fedora he donned reminded Will of something from an old gangster movie. His long and sunken face was clean-shaven, exposing rivers of wrinkles meandering through his weathered skin. A few strands of the stranger's thin gray hair poked from under the hat and danced around in the cold afternoon breeze. But what really grabbed his attention was the man's most striking feature: his sharp blue eyes. Will held them to his own, staring, not able to turn away. He saw something in them, something he couldn't explain. They were deep, knowing, inviting eyes that seemed too beautiful to be housed behind their tired lids. But what was most strange was their familiarity. He couldn't help to feel that he knew those eyes, and had stared at them many times before. Will gaped, wide-eyed, trying to regain his composure.

"Didn't mean to scare you," the man said, his spirited voice breaking the silence.

Will finally caught his breath. "You're the man I saw out here the other day."

"That I am," he replied. "Name's Isaac," he said, offering his hand.

Will took his thin and veiny hand and shook it. He was surprised by the old-timer's strong and sturdy grip, but more so by how warm his hand was. Will relaxed his grip and let his hand go limp in an effort to break the shake. But Isaac continued to squeeze it. Remembering what his father had always said about a man being judged by the strength of his handshake, Will retightened it to meet the stranger's expectations. All the while, Isaac knowingly clutched Will's eyes with his own, making him uncomfortable. Finally satisfied, Isaac nodded, lifted the corners of his mouth up to reveal a warm smile, and relaxed his grip.

"I'm Will Karras."

"I know," Isaac said, still smiling. "Word spreads fast around here. You live in the little house out front."

"Yeah," Will said, a little unsure of himself. "My mom and I just moved here from Rochester."

Neither said anything, but it didn't bother Will. It was something they both shared: don't speak unless you've got something to say. Instead they began walking together, mechanically and without thought. Will stared at the ground ahead of him while Isaac gazed at the landscape of headstones, trees, and clouds. The crunchy brown leaves crackled under the snow as they walked along the edge of the graveyard, carefully avoiding the bodies beneath them. The canal was on their left, lying motionless at the bottom of the hill.

"You were running awfully fast there," Isaac observed, breaking the silence. "Why were you in such a hurry?"

Will stopped and turned toward him, their blue eyes embracing each other. "I guess I was just running," he said with a smile and a shrug. It was Will's turn to ask a question. "Why are you out here?"

Isaac answered with a warm smile and a look that suggested Will should know the answer.

"I guess you're visiting someone?"

"You're right. I've been coming out to visit someone," Isaac offered. Will didn't push the issue, figuring that the old man was probably paying his respects to a wife, friend, or *friends* he'd lost during his long life. The two continued walking toward a tree line at the back edge of the cemetery, and finally came to rest on a marble bench with an inscription that read:

Earth has no sorrow that Heaven cannot heal.

"Thomas Moore if memory serves me correct," Isaac said as he pointed to the words. He closed his eyes peacefully, seemingly vanishing into another time and world. He spoke quietly.

"Here bring your wounded hearts, here tell your anguish;
Earth has no sorrow that Heaven cannot heal."

He opened his blue eyes and aimed them at Will's. "It's beautiful, isn't it?"

Will recognized it as poetry, and, remembering what his eighth grade English teacher had taught him, absorbed the words, playing them over and over in his head in an attempt to find the meaning of the verse. He liked the way poems told a story obscurely, without giving it all away, so that the words could carry different meanings to anyone that read them – even to himself. Poetry was a lot like Will's life as of late: mysterious, deep, ambiguous, and confusing.

He replayed the words, using Isaac's voice to recite them in his mind. "Yeah," he finally answered. "I hope they're true," he added with a shrug.

"That's it!" Isaac burst out excitedly. "You just said the word: *hope*. It's all about hope and faith. If you have one, you've got the other." The old man paused to look at the coming night sky. "Those words, they're true, alright," he added gravely. "I *know* they're true." He smiled. "I know a lot of things – the pain and suffering here where you are right now. But you have to know, and I know, that without pain there is no healing. They go together hand in hand, I'm sure. As sure as you're standing right here." He shifted his gaze to the trees behind Will. "I know you've got pain inside of you – everyone does. *Everyone*. Doesn't matter rich, poor, old, young, buffoons, kings – everyone's got pain." He turned to Will. "You can feel it, now it's time to start healing it."

Will let out a pathetic laugh. "My dad killed himself," he blurted out. The words came out too easily and surprised him. Why was he telling this man – this perfect stranger – one of his deepest secrets? But before his brain could check his mouth he went on. "He left my mom for a younger woman, got all confused, and shot himself in the head." Tears began streaming down his face.

Isaac pursed his lips and bowed his head, silently waiting for the boy to release more of his pain into the frigid winter air.

"He shot himself in the head," he repeated in disgust. Will sniffed and wiped his nose and face with his jacket sleeve. "I don't even know you...and I told you that?"

"Well you've got to tell someone." He paused, frowning and looking down at his feet. "And it's about time you told. But more importantly, it's about time you cried."

He was right. Will hadn't shed a tear since his father's death. Not that night at home when he and his mother got the news, not at the funeral parlor, the wake, the burial, not as he sat alone in his room, not ever.

He regained his composure. "How did you know I haven't cried?"

Isaac lifted his long body up from the bench. He turned his back to Will and stared down into the canal. "For I know the plans I have for you, plans to prosper you and not to harm you, plans to give you hope and a future," he said smiling. "So says the Lord." He turned, and with a wink, breezed by Will. "That one's from the Bible." The air got considerably colder as he walked by. Dumbstruck, Will watched the mysterious stranger slowly stride away and into the darkness.

"Ellen's waiting for you," he called out from the gray dusk. "You better get home."

Will watched him vanish into the nothingness, his black suit absorbing the headstones and trees around him. He began the long walk back toward his house. Questions burst in his mind like popcorn kernels on a hot fire.

CHAPTER 7

MEET THE NEW BOSS

The New York State Chiropractic College campus was less than two miles from Will's house. The campus was beautiful, situated on more than 40 acres of land overlooking Cayuga Lake.

Mrs. Karras worked on the second floor of the main administration building, a light-brown brick structure with long pillars and an impressive concrete staircase in front. Her office was small and cramped with barely enough room for her desk and chair. The windowless cinderblock walls painted a bland white reminded her more of a prison cell than a workspace. It was a far cry from her husband's bright and spacious office – a restored train depot from the early 20th century that she had helped renovate and decorate. It was what it was, she thought. It was a job, but she wasn't thankful for it. She didn't think she should have to work at all, and blamed her dead husband for all of her problems from money and drinking to the decaying house in the cemetery.

Her head swam from the binge of pills and vodka from the day before, making the walk up the two flights of stairs exhausting. Once in her office, she shut the door and opened the top drawer of her desk for a morning shot of courage. She drank the last of her vodka at home and was looking forward to cracking open one of the three airplane-sized bottles she stuffed in there the day before.

They weren't there.

Panic swept over her as she frantically fumbled through pens, *Post-Its*, and paper clips searching for the liquor. "Maybe I put it in another drawer," she mumbled aloud. But the drawers were empty. Her hands shook as sweat beaded on her forehead. She slammed herself down in her chair, defeated, dropped her face to her hands, and began sobbing.

A soft tapping on her door startled her.

"Just a minute," she said, trying to regain her composure. "Come on, Ellen, get it together," she whispered. Wiping her face with a tissue, she stood up, straightened her skirt, and opened the door.

It was Dr. Baker. "Good morning," he said, his bushy dark eyebrows raised as he suspiciously eyed his new employee. His voice was as it had been on the other two occasions she spoke to him: cold and without a hint of compassion. It matched his personality perfectly. He was all business. Those who knew him or worked for him had never seen him crack a smile or laugh. He was always calculated and serious; arrogant, as if he alone carried the solution to some imaginary and impossible puzzle.

"We need to talk," he said, moving his large square frame around her and into the office.

Ellen nodded and turned to face him.

He motioned to the door with a quick jerk of his head. "Shut it."

She did, her hands trembling. His deep-set and dark eyes held her in their gaze, forcing her to look away.

"What's this?" he asked, shaking his head and pointing his fingers at his eyes.

Confused, Ellen touched her hand to her face and held it in front of her. Two of her fingers were smeared with a teary eyeliner paste.

"You look like a clown in a circus," he laughed.

Embarrassed, she reached for the box of tissues on her desk. Dr. Baker intercepted her wrist before she could grab one. He squeezed it firmly.

"What are you doing..." she started, but stopped as he tightened his grip on her. The pain in her wrist throbbed with the rhythm of her quickening heartbeat. He stared at her face, squeezing her frail arm in his vice and watched a tear form, build momentum, and speed down her cheek. And then, just as quickly as he had grabbed her, let her go."

Mrs. Karras seized her wrist with her other hand, and rubbing it stepped away from her desk.

"Get one if you want it," he said, stiffly nodding his head toward the tissue box.

Her arm quaked from a combination of nervousness and pain. She slowly reached to her desk and took one. Smudging more makeup across her cheek, she wiped her face and then tightly clutched the wadded *Kleenex* in her fist.

Dr. Baker stared at the cinderblock wall. "This isn't going to work." His voice was sharp and quick. "I don't like people leaving work because of a," he mimicked quote marks with his fingers, "'headache.'"

"Dr. Baker...I'm sorry, I did have a terrible..."

He turned toward her and cut her off. "No. You didn't. You drink. You drink, you get drunk, you get," again he made the imaginary quotations, "'headaches,' and you leave work early."

"No, Dr. Baker, I...I haven't had a drink in...well, I have a glass of wine once in a while, but I don't drink...really," she insisted. Knowing she was lying, the doctor let her keep talking. "I used to go to winery tours with my husband...we..."

"Oh, your husband. Now there's a good character witness. I know all about Michael. Do you know what his problem was? No discipline," he said, answering his own question. "And you..." He stood up and reached deep into his pockets, his eyes burning into her. The doctor pulled out the missing plastic vodka bottles, and held them in his palm inches under her chin. Mrs. Karras looked down at them and then away, her lips trembling. He grabbed her by the back of the head, and forced her face to his palm. Her body convulsed and heaved with her sobs as he pulled her head back by the hair into its original position.

He raised his voice over her crying, his nose curled and eyebrows constricted into a twisted rage. "My office," he began, speaking slowly between short loud breaths, "my practice...my reputation...my desk...my drawers...my file cabinet...my cinderblocks!" He threw the emptied bottles at her feet and again turned to face "his wall." Within a moment, his breathing became regular, and his voice lost most of its anger. "You are on notice. You have four and a half sick days left this year. Don't call in or leave again unless you are in the same condition as your husband." He brushed past her, put his hand on the doorknob, and turned back around to her. She looked up at him and then back to the floor.

"My son said he met Will yesterday." He shook his head. "Sounds like you've got a real winner there. He'll probably turn out just like his old man."

When he finally left, Ellen Karras crumbled to the floor in a heap, a broken puddle of what she once was.

Unlike his mother's, Will's second day of school was mostly unmemorable. He and Robert met in the lobby, navigated through the subdued morning halls, and walked into homeroom. Both were anxiously waiting for Stanton to walk through the door to see what he would do next. Will breathed a sigh of relief when the late bell rang. Good. He's absent, he thought.

But he wasn't. Thirty seconds later Stanton walked through the door with a yellow tardy slip in his hand. He looked back at Will and waved hello to him on his way to give the pass to Mr. Galero. It wasn't like Robert's wave to him the day before; it was oddly *genuine*. Robert saw the gesture and flashed Will a puzzled look. Will shrugged, confused, and shook his head.

He was on the verge of a panic attack for the remainder of homeroom, but made it through with the help of some deep breathing. When the bell finally rang for first period, Will followed Robert to the door.

"Are you alright? You don't look too good."

"Yeah," Will said, "I'm fine. Why did he wave at me like that?"

Robert shrugged. "I don't know, but knowing him, he's up to something. And it's not good."

The first half of the day passed without incident. Will and Robert sat with Alex and Travis at lunch, only this time Will wasn't facing Stanton's table. Travis kept the group updated. "H-h-he's n-n-not looking at y-y-y-you, Will."

A moment later, "H-h-he's e-e-e-eating h-h-h-his p-p-pizza, Will." And then, "H-h-he's d-d-d-d-d-drink-k-king milk, Will."

"Alright!" Robert snapped. "Enough with the news flashes!"

Travis just stared blankly at Robert. "I w-w-was j-just t-t-t-t-rying t-t-o help."

Will couldn't stop himself from laughing. "It's okay, Travis. I appreciate it, but why don't we just eat now."

Travis smiled and looked down. Robert started laughing, and before long all four of them were laughing uncontrollably. Will's body convulsed every time he thought about Travis's innocent updates. It was the first time he'd belly-laughed in a long time.

Soon the boys calmed down, their contractions coming farther and farther apart.

"W-w-w-hat were we l-l-laughing at?" Travis asked.

The table erupted again and went on until the bell rang for the next period.

Will followed his tablemates to the garbage can and then out into the hall. His mood turned quickly when he caught a glimpse of Stanton ahead of him on his way to the gym. Robert picked up on it.

"Relax. He probably found some other kid to harass."

"Yeah, I kinda doubt that, but hopefully you're right."

"I'll catch you last period."

Maybe Robert was right, Will thought. The laughter had done him good, leaving him feeling more optimistic than he probably should have. Once in the gym, things actually did seem better. The two changed on opposite sides of the locker room, but were put on the same team for basketball. Will only touched the ball once the entire game, and Stanton didn't acknowledge him for the entire period. If Stanton wanted to mock his father's death one day and then ignore him for the rest of his life, it was fine with Will. He had enough drama at home, and didn't need or want any at his new school.

And that's the way it was the rest of the day. Stanton looked the other way when the two boys passed each other in the halls, leaving Will happily disconnected from him. Maybe Stanton Baker had realized the viciousness of his attack Monday morning and couldn't think of anything to top it. "Maybe," he wondered aloud to Robert after school, "Maybe he actually feels bad about what he did."

"I doubt it. But hopefully he's through with you. Maybe he's dreaming up some new plan," he mused. "Like volunteering at the nursing home so he can push the old people in wheelchairs out into traffic."

CHAPTER 8

A TRIP TO VENICE

All things considered, the rest of the week went as well as Will could have hoped. He still felt uneasy going to PE with Stanton without the moral support of Robert, but by Friday even that feeling was subsiding. Since his confusing gesture Tuesday morning, Stanton hadn't made any attempt to communicate with Will at all.

Miss Brick had invited Will to lunch in her office on Friday, and he gratefully accepted. Mr. Larsen brought a pizza from a local deli and apologized for not being able to stay to eat with them. Will didn't know it, but Miss Brick wanted Will to meet him. She knew that he was the kind of positive influence and role model that might be able to help him somewhere down the road. It was also a good excuse for her to see him. The two had been seeing more of each other lately, but just when Miss Brick thought they might get together as a couple, he mysteriously pulled away.

Ellen Karras managed to make it through Tuesday's

trauma, and worked two full days on Wednesday and Thursday. Getting through the workday sober took its toll. She began taking more of her pills during the day to steady her shaky hands and quaking nerves. Dr. Baker made a point of checking up on her, stopping in her office for no reason. Just after lunch one day he actually cornered her near the copy machine and made her breathe on him to prove she hadn't been drinking. But he couldn't follow her home, and within an hour after getting home she was drunk, leaving Will to fend for dinner alone.

He spent his nights in his room, doing his homework, listening to his iPod, or talking to and texting Ian. He missed his friend, and realized he wouldn't be able to hang out with him anytime soon. Only 50 miles separated them, but it might as well have been 1,000 since neither one of them had their license. By now Will knew how his mother would react if he asked her to drive him to Fairport for a weekend, and Ian's mother was working six days a week on a new project. As he lay in bed he shoved the painful thoughts aside, using the sounds of the cars passing by to lull himself to sleep. But his subconscious wasn't as cooperative. His dreams were a theatre of movies starring his father and mother. In one, Dr. Karras sat in a darkened room with a pistol pressed firmly to his head. Another featured his mother clutching an empty bottle as she lay dead in his father's casket. The dreams came often, and Will knew it was the nightly price he would have to pay if he continued to push his feelings away when he was awake.

When he got home from school on Friday afternoon, his

mother was there. It was only 3:00 and already she had her housecoat on. She was flitting around the living room like a moth, clumsily fumbling and rummaging through stacks of boxes strewn across the living room. Her hands shook as she struggled to get the packing tape off of one labeled "KITCHEN." She didn't hear him come in.

Will stopped and stared. She was awkwardly bent over the box, her body twisted and shaking. He didn't recognize her. The heavy drinking and prescription pills coupled with the trauma of her new life were crippling her. She swore at the box, unable to open it, and turned around to find Will gaping at her. *Who are you?* he thought.

Slightly startled but more annoyed she spoke sarcastically. "Hi Will. Glad you decided to make it home." Her face was pale, hiding behind a few strands of unruly and graying hair that dangled over her glazed eyes. The poorly tied housecoat was coming undone at the waist and left her bra exposed. She didn't try to fix it. "Where have you been?"

Will didn't understand the question. "It's Friday. I've been at school all day...you dropped me off there this morning...remember?"

"Noooo," she sang, "You didn't tell me you were going to school today. Don't try to pull that one on me."

Will had never seen her act like this. Her lifeless eyes flashed in anger at him. He stood, silent and still.

"I've been working all day and you have been out running around with your father all over God knows where with God knows who," she said, each word pushing her deeper into hysterics.

Did she just mention her husband? Her dead husband? he thought. She was losing her mind right before his eyes.

As if on cue, his cell phone rang. He cautiously reached down and looked at the screen. It was a text message from Robert asking if he wanted to meet him when he finished his shift at Venice, the pizza place he worked at. The timing couldn't have been better.

"I'll be in my room if you need me," he said, and bounded up the stairs. His mother's bizarre outburst left him numb and depressed. He set his alarm for 8:00 and fell into a deep and dreamless sleep. When the annoying beep sounded, he smacked the snooze button and sat up. For a moment he had forgotten where he was. Darkness filled the room, and he stared in a hazy daze waiting for his eyes to adjust. Reality set back in when he recognized the shadeless window facing the thick brush behind the house. He pulled himself out of bed, grabbed his coat, and went downstairs. His mother was sitting on the couch, smoking.

"I'm going back out."

It was the first time he could remember telling her what he was going to do. In the past, simply out of respect, he would have asked, just because it was the right thing to do. He never wanted to disappoint her, and somewhere buried deep in his mind her voice was always there, guiding him to do the right thing. Unlike some of his friends back in Fairport who were forever angry with and rebelling against their parents, Will realized that he was lucky to have a mom who did so much for him. His friend James went so far as to say that he actually "hated" his mom and dad. Will couldn't understand that. From a young age he had accepted the fact that his parents were not perfect, but that they always did the best they could for him. He realized that they were people just like him – not gods – just ordinary people with problems of their own and children to raise.

Will didn't forget all of that in his moment of defiance. He took his mother's erratic and irrational behavior as a sign for him to take control of the relationship. He had felt more and more lately that their roles were changing, that he was playing the part of the parent while she regressed backwards into the irresponsible teenager. Because of his ability to see things as they really were, he didn't blame her. After all, her entire world had imploded in on her in a matter of months.

Grabbing his wallet from the banister, he headed for the door, leaving his mother frozen like a statue alone and exposed to the weather of her own emotions. He headed past the cemetery gates and onto Bayard Street. The air was heavy and wet, and a cold breeze cut through him as he walked west past the raggedy houses and trailers. His ski jacket, sneakers, and exposed blonde hair were no match for the frigid night air. He walked with his arms straight and stiff, his hands jammed in his jeans pockets for warmth.

Cars passed by, stomping through thick globs of mud-ridden slush that looked more like cookie dough than snow. The reality of Upstate New York weather was all he'd ever known, causing him to believe that 300 cloudy days a year and dirty snow on the ground from October to April were the norm. Even though, in his past life, his family was fairly well off, they never took any trips together to anywhere further than Niagara Falls or

Toronto, just a couple of hours from Rochester. Neither his mother nor father liked traveling, settling for the comforts of home over the uncertainty of a new town.

Crossing the Ovid Street Bridge he found himself at the same corner he had seen the first day he and his mother drove into town. There, still parked in front of the corner bar as if they had never moved, he spotted a group of teenagers. Only this time he recognized them from school.

Their voices died out as soon as they spotted him. He glanced up at the *Filthy McNasty's* sign and then back down to the ground in front of him, partly to protect his face from the wind and partly to divert his eyes from the one person he had hoped not to see until at least Monday morning: Stanton Baker. The boys, about six of them, were huddled together smoking cigarettes. Stanton stood in the center, the focus of their attention.

Once past them, Will quickened his pace. He could feel the boys' eyes on him as they fell in close behind him. They were eerily silent and stealthy, and Will thought that this must be what a helpless wild animal feels like before the hungry lion pounces on it. By the time they reached the middle of town, the silence was snapped by soft whispers that quickly swelled into short bursts of uncontrollable laughter. Will sped up his pace. He could feel Stanton's gang closing the gap between them.

Finally, someone shouted his name. The sound startled him and his body convulsed. The spastic motion brought a roar of laughter from the group. Putting his head back down, he kept up his pace, looking only at the slushy sidewalk in front of him. But just as quickly as he had felt them right behind him, he now sensed that they weren't there anymore. He couldn't be sure, but something told him they were gone. He kept walking, finally working up the courage to turn his head to see if his new nemesis was off his tail. They were nowhere to be seen. He made a quick scan over his other shoulder, but found he was alone.

Will waited for a passing car before crossing Fall Street.

He saw the pizzeria and breathed a sigh of relief. Heat and safety were within sight. His face, hands, and feet had gone numb from the cold, and he had a suspicion that Stanton and his gang hadn't made their last appearance of the night. Through the foggy window he caught a glimpse of Robert sitting at a booth. That's when the first snowball smashed against the side of his face. A burning pain replaced the numbness, and his brain didn't register the cause of it until the second snowball whizzed over his head. He followed its trajectory to the source: Stanton and his thugs were standing under the awning of the florist shop. From what he could see, they had gathered enough ammunition for a full-scale assault. Pre-packed snowballs were scattered at their feet and in their pockets. Running for the safety of the Venice, Will bolted across the street and leapt over the curb using his hands and arms to deflect the onslaught of snowballs that were now bouncing off and flying over him. As he landed on the sidewalk, he felt his lead leg slip from underneath him, sending him crashing to the concrete in front of the pizzeria.

Stanton ran across the street and stood over him. "Oh, man. I didn't mean to make you fall." He sounded genuine and almost concerned. "We were just trying to have some fun. Are you all right?" he asked.

Confused from the fall, Will looked up at the figure over him, wincing in pain. "Yeah," he managed weakly.

"Good. The last thing I'd want to do is to hurt you." He offered Will his hand. "Here, man, let me help you up."

Will took his hand and Stanton pulled him halfway up before releasing his grip and dropping him back to the ground. The back of his head hit the curb bringing a symphony of laughs and shouts of encouragement from Stanton's thugs. Stanton straddled his legs over Will's body. He looked down with a menacing grin.

"You are a loser. Your father was a loser," he paused and squinted. "Hey, you know, you look just like your mother right now. No, really. I was just on top of her too and you both look alike on your backs all twisted up in pain."

Will couldn't speak. His head throbbed. He just wanted to get up, for this beast to go away.

Stanton reached in his pocket and pulled one more tightly packed snowball from his jacket. He cocked his arm back and violently whipped it down into Will's face. The icy ball cracked under his nose, tearing a hole into his upper lip.

Will let out a low moan.

"That's what *she* sounded like, too!" he cackled. Laughing like a hyena, he calmly jogged back toward his hysterical friends, and led them back down Fall Street and into the darkness.

Tears bubbled up from under Will's eyelids, but he stopped them before they had a chance to run down his face.

He put his hand to his lip and saw the blood. When he looked back up, Robert was standing over him, a look of horror on his face. He offered his hand to help him up.

"What the hell happened?"

Will brushed the snow off of his pants and jacket. "I fell off the curb," he said sarcastically.

Robert stared at him in disbelief.

"Stanton happened. Come on, let's get inside before the bell rings for round two."

The empty pizzeria was a long and narrow room with the counter and ovens on the left and a series of booths on the right that extended to the back of the restaurant. Two Italian men with dark eyes and matching thick mustaches stood behind the counter and stared at them when they walked in.

"Roberto, what-a-happened to your friend," one of them asked through his thick Italian accent.

"He fell off the curb," Robert said, and led Will to a secluded booth next to the jukebox.

Gino, the owner, called out from behind the counter. "Roberto!" He motioned Robert toward him and handed him two grease-saturated New York style slices of cheese pizza on paper plates.

Robert walked back to the booth, stopping to grab two Cokes out of the cooler on the way. He slid a plate to Will and the two sat silently together.

"Take this, too," Robert said, handing him a napkin. "For your lip."

Will's lip was still bleeding and was already swollen. He pressed the napkin against the wound.

"What's going on, man? Why do those idiots have it out for you?"

Will shook his head, and sat in silence. His pupils constricted, his fair complexion lost what little color it had as beads of perspiration formed on his forehead, and slowly slid into his pale blue eyes. He dabbed at the sweat with the bloody napkin.

"Drink some Coke," Robert offered, "and relax. Take a couple of deep breaths."

Will obliged and within a minute the symptoms subsided. He felt well enough to eat and bite into the pizza, burning the roof of his mouth as he chewed. "Ahhhhh! Man, that's hot!" Robert held back a laugh. Will took a drink from his glass, and winced in pain as the bubbles from the Coke burned his wounded lip.

It was too much for Robert, and he burst out laughing. "Man, I'm sorry, but you almost have to laugh," he said playfully. "Aren't you psyched that I invited you down here tonight?"

Will started laughing and then gingerly pressed his fingers to his lip to soothe it. "Oh, my lip kills when I laugh!"

Robert bit into his pizza. "What's he got on you?"

"What do you mean?"

"I mean, I've seen Stanton do some terrible things before, but," he paused trying to figure out how to say what he was thinking. "But that gun thing in homeroom and then tonight...it just seems like he's actually got some twisted reason to hate you."

"Roberto!" a voice rang out. "Time-a-to lock up."

On their way out, Gino threw Will a bag of ice for his lip and any other part of his body that needed it. "That-a-Baker boy; next time you-a-kick him in the balls. Works every time."

CHAPTER 9

THE STARS ARE INSANE

The restaurant closed, and the two boys began walking down Fall Street. It was strangely barren for a Friday night, Will thought. Seneca Falls made Fairport look like Vegas.

"Do you want to take the long way around?" Robert asked. "I don't see them at the corner, but they could be hiding."

Will let out a long breath. "You know, man, I'm afraid right now," he admitted. "I'm not used to people coming after me and smashing my face up for no reason."

"I hear ya, let's turn around and take the other bridge -"

"No," Will interrupted. "It's alright. There's not much more he could do to me tonight, right?"

"You really don't want me to answer that. Trust me, he's capable of much worse."

Will rubbed his eyes and shrugged. "Let's just keep

going. We can always try to outrun him. He's kinda fat."

By the time they made it over the bridge, the two boys realized that Stanton was not going to lead another assault. By this time, he and his friends were probably passed out somewhere warm, drunk off a bottle of Dr. Baker's finest scotch.

Robert took Will's mind off his problems for the moment by telling his own bizarre life's story. His father had left him and his mom a little over five years ago, not for another woman, but in pursuit of the ultimate high. "Jonesy" as he was referred to around town, never held down a job for more than six months. It wasn't for lack of motivation; he was just motivated by the wrong things. In high school, Jonesy was an honor roll student and class president. He even got an academic scholarship to Cornell with dreams of one day becoming a pharmacist.

The summer before going away to school, he got a job at the local CVS drugstore as a pharmacy technician. He was basically in charge of giving customers their prescription drugs after the pharmacist had counted and bottled the pills. That's when he began experimenting. Valium, Xanax, Oxycontin – he sampled them all, discreetly a pill here, a pill there. He considered it part of his training. After all, he thought, how could he give a patient a pill without knowing the full effects of the drug?

He probably wouldn't have been caught if not for sampling a new drug, fresh on the scene for erectile dysfunction. When the pharmacist handed him Mr. Durbano's Viagra prescription, he couldn't resist. He stuffed one pill from the bottle into his pocket. When his shift ended, he went home, turned on the TV, and took it. Five hours later, the effects of the drug hadn't worn off yet. The next morning, his mother noticed his discomfort.

"Why are you walking all hunched over like that?" she asked.

Eventually, due to the pain of a 10-hour erection, he confessed. The emergency room doctors found out where he had gotten the pill and turned him in to the local police. He lost his job, his scholarship, and some function of his sexual organ.

After that, things went downhill fast. The magnetic pull of the drugs was stronger than his will. He met Robert's mother when he was 23, and by the time he was 25 he was married to her with a 2 year-old boy in tow.

Menial jobs came and went and their trailer became the local drugstore. In a way, he did realize his dream of becoming a pharmacist – just not the kind of pharmacist his mother could brag to her friends about. It was only a matter of time before he got caught.

One Friday night, after doing ungodly amounts of cocaine, he held up the local *Pick Quick* convenience store. He came away with $135 and three boxes of *Twinkies*. When the police looked at the surveillance video they saw a white male wearing a Buffalo Bills jersey with the nickname, *Jonesy*, boldly embroidered above the number "0". It wasn't a tough case to solve. The State Troopers and local police picked him up at his trailer an hour after the robbery. He was passed out and still wearing his jersey, the money scattered across the floor.

The overwhelming evidence landed him a 12-year armed robbery sentence at the maximum-security prison in Attica. The judge reduced the sentence since the "weapon" he used was a toy *Colt* revolver that Robert used to shoot imaginary Indians with.

By the time Robert had finished his story, the boys were halfway down Bayard Street, the wind now at their backs. Will was impressed with Robert's attitude about the whole thing. He laughed as he recalled his father's complete incompetence in all aspects of his life.

"So you used to smoke a lot of pot?" Will asked.

"Yeah, but I quit a couple of years after my father got sent away." Robert paused and pushed his hands into his pockets. "I didn't want to end up like him. I just saw my mom busting her rear working two jobs and I felt guilty for being a loser...for being like my father."

Will was impressed with Robert's honesty and openness. "My mom is getting messed up a lot now – well ever since my father left us."

Robert waited for Will to continue.

"She's been drinking and taking Xanax." He cupped his hands and blew into them to warm them up. "If you haven't figured it out by now, my father killed himself. It's probably not breaking news to you."

"Yeah, I guess I sort of figured that out."

"In a way I was kind of glad to leave Fairport. Fresh start, all that crap...but I guess you can never shake off your past – especially if Stanton Baker lives in your town." It felt good to get things out in the open, and he knew he could trust Robert to keep it to himself.

The wind had stopped whipping, cleaning the clouds away with it and revealing a starry sky above. The stars were sharp and focused, even through the streetlights.

Just a block before the cemetery, Robert turned to head home for the night. Will took his hand, shook it, and pulled Robert toward him, bumping shoulders in a sign of solidarity.

He looked Robert in the eye. "Thanks," he said.

Robert let out a laugh. "Don't mention it," he said. "I'll give you a call tomorrow. I've got the weekend off. You can spend the night at my house if you want. I'll just make sure its cool with my mother."

Will left Robert, a smile on his face, grateful for his new friend. It was worth the bloody lip to know he could count on someone, he thought.

Walking on autopilot, Will passed his house and slowly strolled back into the depths of the cemetery. It was a nice night, and he didn't feel like going home to face his mother in whatever state she might be in - if she was actually conscious at all. The starlight bounced off the snow illuminating the headstones enough to make out the names. He ended up in the same familiar spot, propping himself up against the black iron fence overlooking the canal. The graveyard didn't creep him out. Surprisingly, it gave him a sense of security that he hadn't been able to find since his father left. He sat moving his gaze from the snow to the markers to the stars, listening to the complete silence found only in the depth of a cold winter's night. If it was snowing, he would have been able to hear each flake as it struck the trees and ground around him. His mind and thoughts were just as quiet and empty as he fixed his gaze on nothing in particular.

The sound of crunching snow jolted him out of his fog, the hypnotic silence cracked by the sound of footsteps. He looked around, alarmed, as it drew closer. Squinting, his heart racing, he made out the form of a person walking toward him.

"Hope I didn't startle you too much," a tired but familiar voice gently called out from the distance.

Will stood in disbelief as he watched Isaac emerge from beyond the gravestones and star-sprayed darkness. The old man was dressed in the same dark suit and fedora.

He smiled at Will, standing face to face with him. "I thought I might find you out here," he said, as casually as if the two were meeting each other for a midday lunch date.

Will was bewildered, his heart still skipping. "What are you *doing* out here?" he asked.

Isaac avoided the question, and instead kept smiling proudly, his pale eyes centered on Will's. "Looks like you got into it tonight," he said, pointing at his own lip to show the flaw in Will's. Without waiting for a response he added, "Some folks just can't let others live their lives. The Baker's have always been like that." He paused, still smiling. "Like father like son, I guess."

Will's face contorted. "How did you know I..."

"'In war the heroes always outnumber the soldiers ten to one,'" he interrupted. His steely eyes still held Will's, but something in his face had changed, his smile replaced with a solemn expression. "You're a soldier, Will, and it's always better to be a soldier than a hero," he added. "Stanton Baker is a hero, but only to those other thugs. Not even in his own mind is he a hero. Somewhere deep inside him he knows that. That's why he does the things he does."

Will could have been one of the headstones, standing still, afraid to move. "But how did you..."

Isaac looked down, moving slowly to his right. He smiled again. "I know you've been struggling, son," he said warmly. "I know because I've struggled with you. You don't deserve the hand you've been dealt, but you've got to play it, and the best way to play a bad hand is to *believe* you can win with it, no matter what the odds are against you." He stopped, winded from the conversation, and sat on an ancient and weathered gravestone of some long-forgotten soul. He erased the smile from his face again, his eyes locked up with Will's. "You've got to *believe* you can win with your hand. Believe in yourself and you'll end up the winner."

"I've never really had to fight anyone before..."

"Uppercut," Isaac interrupted, raising his voice.

Before Will could respond he continued. "It's not about fighting. Hell anyone can win a fight. There's no tree, and I mean no tree that can stand if you cut out its trunk. That's easy, but that's not what this is about. You've been through a lot, and there are people out there who need you to be strong, to believe in yourself again. Your mom's one, but there are others." Isaac lowered his voice. "This – what's happened to you is a test. And it's not over, it's not half over. You're doing fine right now, and you're going to come out fine if you have the will to believe in yourself."

Will stood, stunned. The still night gave up momentarily as the wind blew and rustled his hair and the dead leaves on the trees above them. And then, just as quickly as it came, it died. Will began crying, sobbing in uncontrollable waves from some realization and revelation he didn't fully understand. "I can't," the words escaped his lips before he could stop them. Ashamed, he buried his face in his hands. Isaac stood up and walked over to him, putting his hand on his shoulder. He firmly and fatherly took Will's face in his hands, pulling his head up so the two were looking at each other eye to eye. "You will," he said assuredly.

Will surprised himself and mechanically put his arms around the old man, burying his head in his chest, shocked at the heat radiating out of him on such a cold night. He didn't want to let go of him. Each moment filled him with an overwhelming and inspiring warmth. He felt Isaac begin to shiver, his clothes now as cold as the night itself. Finally unclenching from the old man, he raised his head, filled with an amazing warmth and confidence that grew with each breath from deep inside him. Isaac had given him something. He didn't understand what or how, but that *something*, had changed him in some unimaginable way.

"What did you just give me?" he whispered.

Isaac's voice was shaky, the transfer of energy leaving him exhausted. "I didn't give you anything," he said. "I just lit a match inside of you...just a light to help you find your way a little easier. It's always in there, but we can't always be expected to know which direction to go without a little help."

His voice was tired and raspy. "You're one of the good ones, Will. You haven't deserved everything you've gotten – and things sometimes get worse before they get better. But they will get better. Have faith in yourself. The light's on, now you just need to find your way."

Will stood, stunned, the warmth still pulsing through him. Isaac turned and slowly made his way into the darkness, a shadow within a shadow. Without hesitation, Will turned the other way and headed for home, not saying goodbye or goodnight.

Mrs. Karras was passed out on the couch when he walked in the house and up the stairs to his barren room. He had only unpacked some of his clothes that lay strewn on the floor around the only furniture in the entire room, his bed. But he didn't mind. The move and the week had taken their toll on him, and he knew he would have plenty of time to unpack when his life wasn't quite so hectic. Taking off only his heavy ski jacket, he collapsed into the bare mattress and fell into a deep and dreamless night's sleep.

Morning came and when Will opened his eyes he once again forgot where he was. He looked around, and finally came to his senses, remembering that this was his new room in his new house with his new mother in a new town. The thoughts didn't comfort him, and he closed his eyes for a moment trying to find some reason to like this place. His vibrating cell phone gave him the answer. It was a text from Robert, asking him if he wanted to come over.

It was already noon, and without even taking the time to

shower, Will threw on his jacket and bolted down the stairs. His mother was in the kitchen drinking a cup of coffee and smoking a cigarette.

"Glad you decided to get up today," she said, her voice gruff with a hangover. "I want you to unpack some of these boxes and get your bathroom upstairs scrubbed."

Will turned toward her, still standing in front of the door.

His mother saw his swollen lip. "Come here. What happened to your face?" She was more annoyed than concerned.

He reluctantly walked into the kitchen to his mother. "I met some guys last night and we had a snowball fight. I guess I got hit in the lip." For a split second, he imagined her getting up, pulling a piece of ice from the refrigerator, and gingerly tending to his wound. This time last year she would have made the small cut seem like a lethal gash to an artery. But the second passed and reality came quickly.

"It's about time you made some friends around here." Her voice was ice cold; numb; emotionless. She looked out the kitchen window at the brittle trees in the cemetery. "I didn't think anyone would want to be around you the way you've been acting lately." She took a sip of the hot coffee and snubbed out the cigarette. "It's like your father's personality left his body when he died and got stuck inside you." She pushed herself up from the table. "I'm going to take a shower. Get that stuff done. I'm sick of you lying around here doing nothing."

"Me doing nothing?" He let out a disgusted laugh.

"I'm *trying* to get used to living in a cemetery in a town filled with people who don't like me for some unknown reason. But I'm doing nothing. Look at yourself," he said, blocking her way from the kitchen. "Have you looked at yourself lately? You're a wreck!"

She pushed him out of the way and headed upstairs. "Like I said, you're turning into your father. Nothing's your fault, Will." She stopped at the foot of the stairs. "What's the matter, Will, things not going your way? You used to have it pretty easy, huh? People used to say to me, 'Ellen, what a nice son you have. He's a little quiet, but I wish my son was more like Will.' I wish they could see you now that things are a little tougher. You're not what I thought you were, *son*."

ESTATE SALE

The sarcastic tone in the word "son" sent Will angrily bursting through the door and out into the cold. Any doubt that his mother had flown off the deep end was erased. But his rage was short-lived and quickly replaced with pity. He felt sorry for her.

By the time he made it to Bayard Street, he realized that he had no idea where Robert lived. He pulled out his cell phone to call for directions, but before he could dial a horn caught his attention. It was Travis sitting behind the wheel of a late 70's model Ford F-100 truck. Its body was rusted and the muffler was leaning awkwardly on the pavement. Will jumped a slush puddle and tried to open the door.

"You g-g-g-ot to g-g-g-et in on this s-s-s-side," Travis yelled through the closed window.

Will ran around the back of the back of the beaten truck and climbed in through the driver's side door. "Sorry, that door's b-b-b-roke," Travis apologized.

"No problem, but I can't drive. I'm only 15."

The two boys slid across the bench seat and switched places. Travis gunned the engine and let the clutch out. Will could barely hear the cranked radio over the sound of the broken and dragging muffler. "I alw-w-w-ways f-f-f-orget you guys are y-y-y-ounger than me," Travis shouted.

"How old are you?" Will yelled.

Travis turned the radio down. It still wasn't quiet, but at least they wouldn't have to scream at each other. "S-s-s-event-teen." He smiled at Will anticipating his reaction.

After doing some quick math and realizing Travis would be able to buy beer for his graduation party, Will nodded nonchalantly doing his best to cover his shock.

"I f-f-f-ailed three grades," Travis added seriously.

Will couldn't hide his reaction. His eyes widened in disbelief.

"I'm j-j-just p-p-p-playin', I only f-f-failed twice!" he proudly declared.

The two boys laughed as Travis made an unexpected left turn off Bayard Street. "Where are we going?" Will asked.

"R-r-r-obert's house."

Travis worked the steering wheel hard to keep the truck pointed in a straight line. He turned down a pock-filled road that led to a trailer park. Most of the mobile homes were run-down, one on top of the other like a line of malnourished children crowded in a bread line. But past them, at the very end of the road sat a well-maintained singlewide trailer with a wooden plaque reading "Jones" gently dangling from the mailbox. Travis cut the engine and hopped out. Forgetting,

Will tried his door unsuccessfully and slid across the seat and out into the road.

Robert walked out onto the trailer's small deck in only his boxers and a t-shirt. "I see you had the pleasure of riding in Travis's Ford F'd up 150," he said smiling.

Will laughed and walked up to greet him. "Yeah, that's a smooth ride."

"It's better than w-w-what you guys drive," Travis interjected.

"Relax, Travis," Robert said. "I love the F'd up 150. And besides, its bed will come in handy tonight."

Travis looked puzzled.

"Tomorrow's big item day for the village."

"N-n-no. L-l-last time w-w-we did that w-w-w-we almost got arrested."

"We'll discuss it inside," Robert laughed.

The inside of the trailer was surprisingly roomy. It was cozy; plush carpet supported the comfortable living room furniture and flat screen TV. Robert led the boys to his bedroom. It was still cozy, but just in a teenage boy's room kind of way: clothes – dirty and clean – littered the floor, two guitars lay sleeping on the bed, an amp way too big for his house rested under the small window, and another flat screen TV (bigger than the one in the living room) featured a song list from *Guitar Hero* on it.

Robert moved the real guitars off the bed and pulled the plastic *Guitar Hero* guitar from under the bed. "Do you play?" he asked Will.

"Y-y-you know I'm n-n-no good." Travis said.

"I wasn't talking to you, Travis. I think my cat can play better than you."

"K-k-k-keep that th-th-thing away from m-m-me."

Robert turned to Will. "He's not much of an animal lover. He's afraid of dangerous wild animals like people's dogs and cats."

"I'm n-n-not af-f-f-f-fraid of them...okay," he smiled, "I'm afraid of them. B-b-b-but you w-w-w-would be to if y-y-you always got attacked b-b-b-by them."

"He's convinced that animals – especially dogs – don't like him. He thinks they have something against him because he stutters."

"It f-f-f-freaks them out," Travis said seriously.

Will laughed and sat on the bed. "What's the 'big item' thing you were talking about?"

"N-n-n-no, Robert. We're n-n-not..."

"Relax," Robert interrupted. "I call it an 'estate sale.' Twice a year the village does a big item pickup. Basically, it's a chance for people to get rid of things like refrigerators and couches – things that are too big to go in the regular garbage truck."

Will reached for the plastic guitar and picked it up. "What's that got to do with an estate sale?"

"You'll see tonight."

"N-n-no he w-w-w-won't. You n-n-need my truck and I'm n-n-not going to l-l-let you use it."

Robert looked at Will and smiled. "He'll let us use the truck." He turned to Travis. "I'll buy you dinner tonight... from Venice."

"But y-y-you get free f-f-food from there."

"Right! But you don't. Therefore, technically I'm buying you dinner." He turned to Will sensing his apprehension at the mention of going back downtown to the sight of the beating the night before. "Don't worry, Will. They deliver."

The boys spent the afternoon in the confines of Robert's room playing video games. Robert and Will made it through the Slayer song on the hard level while Travis struggled to get past *Barracuda* on easy. As promised, Robert treated his guests to two large pizzas from *Venice*.

The day created a great diversion for Will. He didn't have to think about his mother, and decided he would spend the night at Robert's house with or without her permission. In a way, Will wanted her to call him just so he could ignore the call. But she never did.

At around 10:00 Robert announced that it was time for the estate sale. Travis objected, but Robert reminded him that unless he was willing to vomit the contents of his stomach, he was in. As the boys piled into the truck through the driver's side door, Robert reminisced about past estate sales. "Most of the stuff we find is junk from the 80's. Last year we even saw a TV that had a knob to turn the channels! Man, can you imagine how bad it would suck if you didn't have a remote and had to get up to turn the channel?" Still unsure of the purpose of their quest, Will gazed out the window at dead refrigerators, stoves, and gaudy and twisted furniture littering the curbsides.

"Pull over," Robert ordered Travis. The truck lumbered

to a stop right in front of a puke-green ripped and torn couch. "It's perfect! Let's go!"

The three boys poured out of the truck and quickly heaved the couch up and into its bed. They shook their cold hands and piled back into the cab. "What are we going to do with that?" Will asked. Robert began laughing and then Travis joined in, neither boy giving up their secret plan.

Travis turned off of Bayard Street into the meandering depths of the village. "Good idea," Robert commented. "Stay off the main streets." The next stops yielded a weathered coffee table and a faded yellow chair. "That's g-g-g-goood," said Travis. "Let's s-s-set it up."

"No," Robert said scanning the streets. "Not yet."

Travis steered the car down Bayard Street and onto Cayuga. Robert applauded him. "Good thinking. The rich people always have the best stuff out." Just past the school they spotted the Holy Grail: a wood-framed 32-inch television complete with cracked screen. "Pull over!" Robert demanded.

Traffic was light, but the boys had to work fast so they wouldn't be seen. They piled out of the truck and lifted up the TV. It was slippery and crusted with a coat of wet snow, but they managed to throw it into the bed without incident. The tired shocks moaned under the weight of the new prize.

"W-w-where's the s-s-sale going to b-b-be, Robert?"

"I think the Baker house would be perfect for these treasures."

Will turned quickly to Robert. "Stanton's house?" The idea, even though he didn't know what they were going to do, filled him with a mixture of fear and exhilaration.

"Yes!" Travis exploded, now fully behind the plan.

He carefully guided the overfilled truck down Cayuga Street and then through back streets until they finally arrived at an upscale new housing development. Unlike Cayuga Street, the houses here were without history or character. They were stacked neatly and uniformly among one other. There were no sidewalks, and the trees were small and immature. It was a perfect place for Stanton to live, Will thought.

The Baker house was the last on the cul-de-sac where the street ended. A quick shot of claustrophobia swept through Will as he realized there was only one way out. Two yard lamps brilliantly lit up the white two-story house. Travis pulled over in front of it and cut the engine.

"Okay, here's the deal," Robert said, fastening his gloves. "We've got to work fast. That's Dr. Baker's BMW so we know someone's home." He turned to Will. "Just follow our lead and be as quiet as you can."

They poured out of the truck again and stealthily moved to the back of it. Robert undid the gate. "No!" Travis warned. It was too late. The gate swung on its broken hinges and crashed to the street. Robert and Will looked up stunned. "I b-b-broke it when I b-b-backed into the gas pump last week." Will erupted in a contagious burst of uncontrollable laughter. Robert and Travis joined in until the three were gasping for breath. Robert finally contained himself. "Come on, we'll deal with that later. Grab the couch first."

Travis jumped into the bed and grabbed one end of the couch. Robert took the other side while Will guided it out of the truck. "We got this one," Robert told him. Will watched the boys waddle through the snow to the middle of the Baker's front yard, wheel it around so it would be facing the road, and drop it. "Will, grab the table," Robert ordered. Will pushed the coffee table off the bed and with Travis's help, set it neatly in front of the couch. Robert ran past them with one of the broken floor lamps in his hand. He carefully placed it next to the sofa. "Perfect," he whispered loudly.

Will was beginning to understand, and he worked with the others until they had a complete living room set in the Baker's front yard. Each piece had its own space, and under Robert's management, they had created a virtual furniture showroom-perfect ensemble. Will began cackling with pleasure as he admired their creation. "Alright, let's get the tailgate and get the hell out of here!" Robert said. It took all their strength to lift it into the bed, but they managed, and jumped back into the cab.

Travis took the wheel, started the engine, and attempted to U-Turn the old Ford in the narrow street. There wasn't enough room. He'd have to back it up and make a K-Turn. Nervously, he backed the truck up. He was mumbling to himself in an effort to stay calm, and was doing fine until his foot slid off the clutch. The truck bucked backwards and into a short ditch in the Baker's front yard. He shifted into first and gunned the engine. The back tires spun, unable to get enough bite to move the truck. He tried again and again until the back tires were spitting snow and mud into tall rooster tails behind them. The excitement coursed through Will and he began convulsing with laughter. "It's not f-f-f-funny," Travis yelled. But his speech impediment only made it funnier to Will. Robert joined in and between laughs asked, "What the heck are you doing?"

"You know I f-f-f-failed my d-d-driver's test twice b-b-because I couldn't K-K-K-Turn," Travis said angrily.

Robert and Will couldn't control themselves. Travis was in a panic. "G-g-get out and lock the hubs!"

"Alright, alright. Move so we can get out of this crap box," Robert said.

Travis grappled with the door handle, but it wouldn't budge. "It's s-s-stuck! Jump out the w-w-w-window!"

Will frantically rolled down the window and the two boys crawled out. Robert stumbled through the snow to the back wheel so he could lock the hubs and put the ancient truck into 4-wheel drive. Will watched Robert's movements and ran to the other back wheel to lock that hub. Fortunately he was a quick study and deftly locked the wheel into position. He ran to the other front driver's side wheel and locked that one into place, but Robert was having trouble with his side. "I can't get this one!" he yelled.

Will ran over to help, but something was wrong with the hub. "T-t-twist it...oh forget it!" Travis said and dropped out of his window with a thud. The three boys were fumbling with the wheel when they saw the porch light from the Baker house illuminate. "Crap! Someone's coming!"

Travis continued working while Robert and Will climbed back into the truck to see if they could move it. Robert took the wheel, put the truck in gear, and gunned the engine. The tires spat slush, covering Travis in the sloppy mix. From the side-view mirror, Robert saw Dr. Baker emerge from the house holding the family pet, Rex, a 95-pound Rottweiler, by the collar. Robert's voice shuddered in a nervous but excited laugh. "He's got the dog! Travis is going to freak!"

Dr. Baker saw the living room set in his front yard and a maniacal smile crossed his lips. "I got you sons of bitches," he hissed. "Rex, voraus! Voraus!" The dog, obviously trained in German tore off after the truck and zeroed in on Travis. Dr. Baker yelled, "Braver hund, braver hund!"

"Holy crap, the dog's a Nazi too!" Robert said. He gunned the engine and popped the clutch. The tires gripped and the truck lurched forward and out of the ditch. Travis, covered in slop, tried to jump into the moving truck's open passenger side window. Robert stopped and Will grabbed his arm to help him in, but Travis couldn't keep his balance on the slippery road and fell. Rex closed in on his prey and, just as Travis picked himself up, tackled him back to the ground. The dog's teeth gnashed into Travis's jacket, tearing out a huge chunk. Travis stripped off the coat and Will looked on in disbelief as the dog violently thrashed the helpless clothing back and forth like a wounded squirrel. Travis climbed up the side of the pickup bed. Robert revved the engine and took off down the road with Travis's legs still dangling over the side. Rex released the jacket and tore off after the truck, his eyes sharply focused on one of

Travis's dangling feet. The muscular animal accelerated faster than the truck and the dog caught up and bit into Travis's right boot. He let out a scream and lifted his left leg over and into the bed, but the dog wouldn't let go. As the truck sped up Rex dug his teeth in deeper, dropped his hind end to the street, and like a water-skier on a lake, glided on his backside down the slippery road. With all the effort he could manage, Travis shook his leg wildly, finally breaking the dog's grip. Rex gracefully slid to a stop as Travis flopped onto his back in the safety of the rusty truck bed.

By the time they made it back to the safety of Robert's house, Travis was numb with cold and the two boys in the cab were out of breath from laughing the entire trip. Travis wasn't as amused. "I c-c-could have been k-k-killed by that animal!" he yelled as Will helped him out of the bed. But by the time they were inside the warm confines of Robert's trailer he had calmed down.

"You gotta admit," Robert said with a grin, "it was the best estate sale we've ever had."

"Yeah, b-b-but you owe me a n-n-new j-j-jacket!"

WRESTLING WITH THE DEVIL

Feeling guilty about running out on his mother the day before, Will called her three times on Sunday morning. Each time her phone went straight to voicemail. He knew she was home, and pictured her passed out on the couch, still unconscious from last night's binge.

Will thought about going home to check in on her, but when Robert's mother offered to take the boys to Rochester to the Eastview Mall, he gratefully accepted. He knew there was nothing he could do for his mother, and thought a trip back to his old turf might help take his mind off of things. Travis decided that a hot shower and nap in his own bed would do his battered body more good than a long day walking around the mall.

It turned out that Will was right. The mall was a great diversion from his troubles, and he and Robert had a fun-filled day "accidentally" bumping into pretty girls and demoing new video games. Will even got to introduce

Robert to one of Rochester's greatest treasures: The Garbage Plate. It was a gastrointestinal nightmare created by a Greek immigrant, Nick Tahou, in 1918. His restaurant bore his name and his famous creation consisted of two cheeseburgers, macaroni salad, home fries, raw onions, and some sort of meat sauce all thrown on top of each other and served with Italian bread and butter on a paper plate. Will had only been to Tahou's a couple of times with his father when he was younger, but ate a similar "trash plate" at a diner near his school in Fairport every week with Ian. One of the food court restaurants had their own version of a Garbage Plate, and even though it wasn't quite as good as the original, it satisfied his hunger for home.

Robert ate his in record time. "I think I might get another one for later," he said leaning back in his chair.

"No, you don't have to. The great thing about a plate is that you keep burping it up for hours. It's the meal that keeps on giving."

For Will the only thing that would have made the day better was if Ian could have spent it with them. Will texted him to see if he could meet up with them, but his mother was working so he was stuck at home without a ride.

The day went by too fast, and it was after 7:00 when Robert and his mother dropped Will off at his house. He expected his mother to be angrily waiting for him, throwing questions about where he'd been for the past day and a half. Somewhere not too deep inside of him he *wanted* her to yell at him just so he knew she still cared. Instead he found her asleep on the couch dressed in the same frumpy housecoat he left her in the day before. The dark house reeked of stale cigarette smoke and alcohol. Disappointed and exhausted, Will plodded up the stairs, ripped off his clothes, and collapsed into his bed and off to sleep.

The alarm sounded, waking Will to a new week. The weekend had left him a bit more optimistic about his new life in Seneca Falls. It pushed Stanton Baker to the back of his mind, and the thought of the estate sale brought a smile to his face. He jumped in the shower and ran downstairs into the kitchen where he poured himself a glass of milk.

"Mom!" he yelled, expecting her to either be in her bedroom or still in the shower.

"I'm in here," she growled from the living room.

Will turned toward the voice to find his mother eerily peeking over the back of the couch at him. Her eyes were dark, like someone had pressed them with a bingo blotter. He could only see the top of her head down to the sunken shadows of her eyes. Shocked at her appearance, he lifted his eyebrows and quietly asked if she was alright.

She sat up, exposing an expression Will had never seen from her before: eyes wide, nose curled, the corners of her lips turned up. She sat there momentarily, locked in the clown-like pose. Nodding, her voice morphed into a hoarse whisper. "Of course I'm fine, *Will*. Why wouldn't I be fine, *Will*. Your father blew his brains out onto a wall, but I'm fine, *Will*. I'm in debt up to my ass, but I'm fine, *Will*," her voice swelled with each word. "I'm living in a cemetery, but I'm fine *Will*," she said, and began violently pulling strands of freshly grayed hair out of her head.

But then, just as quickly as it had started, her voice fell into a gentle whisper. Her eyes softened and she began to sob. "I can't get it out," she said, stroking her hair. "I want to dye it, but I'm afraid it will just come right back. It's everywhere," she finally finished, closing her eyes and collapsing back to the couch.

Will walked toward her, calm, unafraid, and unashamed, surprising even himself. It's not the way he should have reacted to her, he thought, but it felt *right*. He was in control, not of the situation, but of himself. His heart was steady, his thoughts calm, as he moved the empty prescription bottle and set it on the coffee table. He closed his eyes, took a deep breath, and hugged his mother. She was already asleep by the time he released her, and he gently lifted the afghan she had knitted some twenty years ago up from her waist and tucked it under her chin. He kissed her forehead, whispering, "Things will get better," and headed for the door.

The day was cold, but for the first time in a long time the sun was shining, blindingly bright. Will watched the squiggly lines dance in front of his eyes as he made his way out of the cemetery and down Bayard Street. Walking to school, he thought about his mother. She was taking too many pills, drinking too much, and her psychotic episodes were beginning to scare him. Isaac's voice replayed in his head, "In the end, things will be okay."

A blowing car horn stole him from his thoughts. Robert's mother sat smiling behind the wheel of their salt-rusted two-door blue Toyota Tercel. Robert motioned to him, and he ran to the car, leaping over the plowed mush hanging over the edge of the curb. Will climbed into the cramped back seat, happy to see his friend and a smiling mother.

Her expression changed. "Your lip looks a little better," she said. Will had forgotten about his injury until she mentioned it. "I didn't want to be nosy yesterday, but…"

Robert huffed like he had sprung a leak. "Stanton Baker is what happened to his lip," he said. "She didn't want to be nosy," Robert added sarcastically to Will, before explaining the ambush and the final cheap shot from Stanton.

His mother pinched the bridge of her nose, shaking her head in disgust. "I know I shouldn't say anything," she began.

"But…" Robert interrupted playfully.

She let out a laugh, eyeing Robert suspiciously. "But," she continued, "that boy needs someone to knock the crap out of him."

It wasn't what either boy expected to hear, and they both laughed in unison. It was always funny when a parent – especially a mother – spoke like that in front of their kids.

"Mom, that's not very Christian," Robert mocked playfully. His mother was a permanent fixture at the local Catholic Church.

She laughed. "I know it's not, but evil is what evil is and that boy is evil. He's just as bad as his father," she said.

Will's ears perked up now that she mentioned Dr. Baker, his mom's boss. "What about him?" he asked.

They were almost to the bridge, passing the IGA food store on their left. "Stanton's father was always a very smart man – I mean back even before he was your age everyone knew that he was some sort of a genius." She turned right over the bridge. "His father was a family doctor, a nice man – they say the apple doesn't fall far from the tree, but it did in this case. Old Doc Baker treated my family more than once when we didn't have any insurance or money to pay him. Well it came to be known later that Stanton's father – Douglas – took to stealing his father's medicines." They stopped for the light next to Filthy's. "Most kids would have stolen some kind of drug to get themselves high, but Douglas was, like I said, real evil. He took the drugs, all sorts of different ones, and stored them in the shed behind the house. Then he started trapping neighborhood cats, imprisoning them in small cages, sometimes two or even three in one cage, in the shed with the medicine." She took a deep breath, not wanting to reveal the next part of the story. "That's when he started doing the," she took her hands off the wheel momentarily to form quotes with her fingers, "'experiments' on the animals."

Will's face curled up in disgust and his stomach rolled over on itself.

Robert's mother turned left off of Cayuga Street and onto Beryl Ave. bringing the school into view. "He started injecting and dusting the cats' food with crazy mixtures, creating concoctions just to see how they affected the animals." She paused, waiting behind a Chevy Suburban in the car rider line, took a deep breath, and continued. "Most of the cats died, but some were left paralyzed or crippled, only to die later. They would have been better off dying right away, poor creatures. It makes me sick just thinking about it." The car inched forward as they neared the drop-off point. "The police found out and charged him with cruelty to animals. Doc Baker got the charges dropped – I know he hated to bail his kid out, but he couldn't stand to see his son sent to jail. Stories went around town that Douglas kept messing with animals out in that shed," she sighed. "He failed out of medical school after his first semester, and ended up going to chiropractic school. He's some sort of a big shot now down at the Chiropractic College."

Will and Robert climbed out of the car. "Thanks for the uplifting story," Robert said sarcastically.

"You guys have a good day today," she said before the door closed behind them.

As the boys neared the entrance, Will, his head high and focused on the door ahead said, "That guy's my mom's boss."

Robert shook his head. "Great," he said.

Will's eyes were intense, still looking straight ahead. "Yeah. I wonder what kind of stuff he's pulling on her. She's been way worse since she started the job. I kinda thought it was stress from everything she's been through, but having *him* as her boss definitely doesn't help," he said.

Will caught a glimpse of his nemesis just as the two boys sat down on a bench in front of the school's trophy case. He and a group of his cronies were looking over at Will and laughing. But the looks and laughing didn't have the same effect on Will that they would have the week before. He met Stanton's gaze calmly, his head still high, their eyes locked together. Stanton sensed some change in Will's stare. It wasn't the same. The fear was gone, making Stanton uncomfortable. Not wanting to or being able to afford to back down, Stanton nudged one of his friends, whispering something to him. Soon the whole group was staring at Will.

The homeroom bell broke the standoff, and soon an army of teens in full early morning zombie mode trounced together to their lockers. Stanton's gang was behind him, and Will, filled with a new sense of confidence, walked to his locker. He could feel himself shedding his old skin and slowly squeezing into one that fit much more comfortably.

Once in homeroom, Mr. Galero greeted him with a whopping, "Hi, Will!" complete with a full-tooth grin under his dark mustache. Hearing his effeminate voice brought a smile to Will's face, and he quietly returned the greeting. Stanton entered a moment later, but to Will's surprise, didn't even look back in his direction. Robert took his seat next to Will.

"I wonder if they got the furniture out of their yard," Robert whispered with a smile.

"I just hope Travis didn't go back to ask them for his jacket back," Will replied laughing.

The day was uneventful, and Will didn't see Stanton again until lunch. Robert and Will joined Alex and Travis at their usual table. "He must not know it was us," Will guessed, carefully eyeing Stanton and his goons. They spent the rest of the period happily replaying Saturday night's estate sale to Alex. "I wish I was there," Alex said between bites of his sandwich.

"No you d-d-d-don't!   That d-d-dog could have swallowed you whole," Travis scolded. Then, turning to Robert, "Y-y-you still owe me a new j-j-jacket."

The bell rang and Will made his way to the gym. Coach Barnes, a tall, shaven-bald man in his mid 40's, stood in the locker room doorway talking to Stanton. He was a typical high school PE teacher who considered himself a coach first and a physical education instructor last. An all-conference linebacker in high school, Coach Barnes fell between the cracks at the division III college he went to, becoming just another face on the team. At Mynderse, he spent the majority of his time during the season looking at film and preparing for Friday night's game. He kept busy in the weight room with his boys during the off-season. He seemed ordinary and predictable, and looked like he could have worked at Will's old school in Fairport or any other school in the country.

But looks can be deceiving. Unbeknownst to Will, Coach Barnes was one of Dr. Baker's closest friends. The two had gotten to know one another shortly after Barnes moved to Seneca Falls and needed his back tweaked. Their relationship flourished when they both realized they shared the same hobbies: golf, boating, drinking, gambling, and womanizing. Because of his close ties with Dr. Baker, the coach treated Stanton more like a friend than a student. It was fairly well-known throughout the school that Stanton used Barnes as one of his connections to buy him beer and liquor.

Stanton stopped his conversation and stepped in front of Will just as he was walking past them. Will's heart began racing, and he tried to step around his foe. Stanton shuffled to the side, blocking his path, and wickedly stared into his eyes. Will looked down and tried to move past him again, but this time Stanton firmly put his hand on Will's shoulder and pulled him toward him. "Tell your retarded friend Travis that I have something for him," he whispered in his ear. And then he added, "You're mine today." The voice sent shivers down Will's spine. Stanton knew who was behind the estate sale.

Will's head was spinning. He tried to think of some reason not to dress out for the class, but knew that Barnes would make him. He reluctantly and mechanically found a locker, pulled off his jeans, and slipped his shorts over his legs. He scrambled to get into his squad line before the tardy bell rang. He didn't need to draw any more attention to himself than was absolutely necessary. Will stood at the back of his line, twisting and lifting his head during the warm-up stretches in an effort to keep an eye on his nemesis. But Stanton wasn't in his line. He stood up, arms burning from the 10 required push-ups, and couldn't believe what he saw: Stanton was still talking to Coach Barnes except now he was wearing gym shorts and Travis's jacket. The two caught Will's gaze and smiled.

The warm-ups over, Coach Barnes finally sent Stanton back to his line and ordered two of his varsity football players to unroll the wrestling mats from the foot of the bleachers. "Booooys," he bellowed, authoritatively stretching out his words for dramatic effect. "Today we'll start a unit on wreeeestliiiing." The boys' reactions reflected their body type; the weak kids cringing while the strong licked their lips. Will noticed Stanton and a few of his friends watching him as the football players finished unrolling the mats. Stanton, still sporting the dingy winter jacket, nudged one of his stooges in a "watch this" motion. He pointed at Will and mouthed the words he had whispered to him earlier, "You're mine." The scene generated a big laugh from his audience. *It doesn't take a genius to figure out what's coming*, Will thought as he added up the clues from Stanton quietly talking to Coach Barnes to the wrestling mats that now lay before them.

"Karras," the coach said, his voice and face softening. He motioned Will toward him. Will walked over to him and cowered under the powerful man's touch as he put his hand on his shoulder.

"You're from Fairport," he said loud enough for only Will to hear him. Will nodded. It was the first time he had spoken directly to him since he'd been at Mynderse. The coach forced a crooked smile and his eyes narrowed. "They beat us pretty good in sectionals last year," he said. His fake smile disappeared. "You'll be wrestling Baker today," he said, satisfied, and then shouted, "Baker!" Stanton came forward.

"Yes sir," he said, already knowing what Coach Barnes was about to tell him.

The coach grinned, his large hands filling his training pants pockets. "You'll be wrestling Mr. Karras in the first match today," he said.

Stanton smiled, while Will, realizing he was part of a

set-up, sighed in disgust. The coach heard him. "What did you say to me, Karr-ass?" he demanded, purposely stressing the second syllable in the name.

The football players laughed at the clever twist on his name. Will moved his gaze to the mat, seeing it now as a target on Stanton's shooting range. There was no way out. No matter what he said, Coach Barnes would twist his words, gestures, or silence into something it wasn't and turn the scene into a bigger fiasco than it was already going to be. He knew he was trapped. He stood frozen, still staring at the mat.

The coach exploded. "Look at me when I'm talking to you!"

The outburst got the attention of the entire class. The football players again exchanged glances and giggles in expectation of what was to come. They had heard that voice before at practices and games, and were glad that this time it wasn't directed at one of them.

Will raised his eyes up to the tall bald man. His heart pounded and sweat dripped from beneath his arms. He could smell the fear spewing from his pores.

The coach crouched down, hands on his knees, and moved within inches of Will's face. His voice was a rabid whisper. "Guess where I was Saturday night?"

Will shook his head quickly, not sure what to make of the question.

"You don't know? I saw you. You mean you didn't see me?"

Will couldn't find his voice so he shook his head again.

The coach forced another smile before his face settled stone serious. "I was at Dr. Baker's house Saturday night. You ruined our party."

Will's eyes widened and his jaw dropped.

"There's no way out of this one. Not unless you're going to be like your old man. You don't have a pistol and a bullet tucked into your shorts, do you? Now get out there on that mat and take what you deserve, and take it like a man."

Trembling, Will nodded and dejectedly stepped to the center of the circle. Coach Barnes took Stanton by the arm and gently pulled him to his side. "Anything goes," he whispered. "I won't see a thing. You do what you need to do to him."

Stanton nodded and smiled in satisfaction, and, still wearing Travis's coat, made his way to the center of the mat. Squaring his body to Will's, he cracked his neck from side to side, bouncing like a boxer before a prizefight.

Will stood limply at the center of the mat, and thought about Stanton's Judo training. He prepared himself for the worst.

CHAPTER 12

JACOB

J acob Larsen was a successful local businessman/ philanthropist who donated as much time as he did money to the local community. He was a tall and handsome man in his mid-40's with penetrating blue eyes and thick blonde locks of hair. Born poor in Oil City, a struggling small town in western Pennsylvania, he worked his way through college, earning a Bachelor's degree from a small private college in Rochester. It was there that he met Sarah, the girl that would become his wife. The two were married in the summer following their college graduation, and moved into a modest house in Fairport where, within a month, they found out she was pregnant. Jacob spent his days writing for and editing local magazines and newspapers. The pay was bad and the work inconsistent, but he wanted to do something with his gift: writing. He dreamed of one day supporting his family, working from home writing and editing books, but realized that for the time being it was only a dream. Jacob understood that his hard work would eventually pay off, but in the meantime he would have to work nights and weekends at a local supermarket chain, collecting and sorting recycled aluminum cans.

Sarah's pregnancy was uneventful up until the night she went into labor. For fourteen hours she struggled before the doctors decided to perform a C-section. They couldn't stop the massive hemorrhaging and she bled to death soon after giving birth to a healthy baby boy. Cracked but not broken, Jacob put the baby up for adoption, knowing that he couldn't give his child the life he deserved. Wanting to get away from the city and its memories, Jacob moved into a modest house on Cayuga Lake in Seneca Falls where he started a small publishing company specializing in children's literature. His big break came when he took a chance on a young author from Brooklyn whom he'd met at a convention. Spending more than two years and his entire life savings on publishing the project, The Chapel Street Basement series was born. The first book, *Hammet's Revenge,* sold over one million copies worldwide. He was financially set for life, but wanted to give back to the kids that bought his books.

That's when he began volunteering at the local K-8 school, Cady Stanton Elementary. It was there that he met Miss Brick. The two were immediately attracted to each other, but each thought the other wasn't ready for a relationship. Larsen knew that she had just gone through a brutal divorce, and although it had been 10 years since his wife died, Miss. Brick thought that he would make his move toward a relationship when he was ready. They hung together in limbo, both secretly wanting and waiting for the mysteries of love to fall into place. Their magnets would sporadically pull them toward each other, but always mysteriously and inexplicably flipped at the last moment, leaving an invisible and impenetrable force between them.

Their love of kids was the cement that bonded their relationship. Both shared a passion for the students, injecting confidence and hope into those who needed it most. Students trusted them with their problems, and craved their non-judgmental advice. Fueled by their occasional get-togethers for dinner or baseball and basketball games, rumors that the two were "seeing" each other bounced through the halls. But, at least for now, they were just rumors.

The students looked forward to seeing Larsen's warm and inviting face and hearing his encouraging words. Each year he published a book of student work, and donated the money it raised back to the school. And when the baseball team needed a middle school coach, he offered his services again, and had been doing it ever since.

While he loved the camaraderie of coaching the team, watching the kids get better, feeling the highs and lows of an entire season, he dreaded tryouts and cuts. Unfortunately, there was no way around it, and each year in March he'd have at least 20 kids show up for tryouts. Of those 20, at least seven (sometimes more) had never even played baseball. They just wanted to be around him. He was known throughout the school and community, liked by both parents and students, a rarity in any school environment. Mr. Larsen, or "Larsen" as the kids called him, had that special quality of making people feel comfortable, and more importantly, making them feel wanted. He treated the young people with respect, and actually considered the young humans "human."

Stanton tried out for the team in the 8th grade, and he was not a good ball player. He was slow, had little stamina, and had not played baseball since he was in the Pee Wee league as a nine year-old. Unlike some of the other boys who tried out just to get the chance to spend time with Larsen, Stanton didn't care about him. Dr. Baker poisoned his son's opinion of the man. "He's probably a little funny," he would say. "You know, probably queer. That's why he's not married." Or worse still, he sometimes implied that Larsen did so much work with the middle school boys because he was attracted to them. "It's not right for a single man his age to spend so much time around young men. He's as straight as a boomerang."

The feeling was mutual. While volunteering at the elementary school, Jacob witnessed Stanton's cruelty firsthand. He saw how he treated some of the less popular kids, and resented his smug and arrogant personality. Larsen prayed that he didn't have Derek Jeter's skills so that his decision to cut him would be an easy one. On the first day of tryouts, the chubby boy came onto the field decked-out like a major leaguer. Sure that his son wouldn't get cut, his father had outfitted him with a new glove, bat, baseball pants, and a $200 pair of cleats. But it didn't take long for Larsen to see that his appearance was the only thing resembling a major leaguer. He couldn't catch, had an awkward and weak throwing arm, and was the slowest kid on the bases. Stanton didn't survive the first round of cuts.

Like most kids who tried out and didn't make it, Stanton didn't understand why he got cut. He suffered from what Larsen privately referred to as "delusional greatness." Some children, no matter how bad they were, just couldn't believe they weren't going to make the team. Dr. Baker couldn't believe it either.

Larsen knew of Dr. Baker from seeing him in passing, but had never actually met the man. He did know of his reputation, and that he had never seen him smile. Larsen always waved pleasantly at him – sometimes a bit overzealously – just to see if he could erase the scowl from his face. He couldn't. Dr. Baker, he guessed, was one of those people that took life too seriously. His recipe for life didn't include much compassion, humility, or humor.

The night Stanton got cut, Dr. Baker called Larsen at home. His voice was cold. He demanded to know why his son didn't make the team. "I know it's political over there," he said, barely restraining himself from shouting. *Political?* Larsen thought. *The man with the reputation of having all the slimy characteristics of a politician is calling me political?* He calmly explained that that wasn't how he operated, and that Stanton got cut because he just wasn't as good as the other kids trying out.

Dr. Baker couldn't and wouldn't accept that answer, and by the end of the call was maniacally yelling into the phone. "Do you know how much money I spent on his gear? Over $500," he roared, answering his own question. "The bat alone cost $150. My son does not get cut from anything, and you *will* hear from me again. I'd watch my back if I were you," he said slamming his phone shut.

Larsen shrugged the threat off, chalking it up as another disgruntled and unappreciative parent that would get over it. But Dr. Baker didn't "get over it." He was a man of his word, or in most cases, a man who followed through with his abusive threats. It was another ingredient of his pitiful personality.

Even if Larsen had heeded the warning and "watched his back," he wouldn't have been able to predict or stop what happened next. A week to the day after the phone call, the doctor and his son stealthily pulled up to Larsen's house in his new BMW. There was a PTA meeting at 7:00, and Dr. Baker knew that they couldn't begin without their treasurer, Mr. Larsen. Dr. Baker cut the lights of his car before entering the driveway and waited under the canopy of the night sky for him to come out. When they saw the house lights go dim, the Baker's, as if they were starring in a cheesy Hollywood action movie, put on a set of matching black ski masks and crept onto the front porch.

Larsen never knew what hit him. As he opened the door, Dr. Baker coiled his body and masterfully spun, released, and delivered his shin directly into Larsen's knee. His timing was perfect. The bone on bone impact produced a sickening crunch sound followed by an agonizing groan. Larsen instantly collapsed into a broken pile on the porch. Stanton seized the moment and jumped on top of him, throwing his sharp elbows into Larsen's skull and face. He was unconscious and bleeding badly. Dr. Baker pulled his son off of their victim, reached down, and carefully wedged a baseball under his chin. It was a calling card of sorts, the doctor's twisted way of being sure Larsen knew who attacked him.

The wounds sent Mr. Larsen to the hospital for more than two weeks. The assault left him with a shattered knee, a severe concussion, and various cuts and bruises on his face and head. He wanted to press charges against the Bakers, but with no witnesses and only a baseball as evidence, there was nothing the police could do. When the police questioned the doctor about the crime he called his lawyer and threatened to sue the police force for harassment if they talked to him about it again. As added insurance, he called the mayor, an old drinking buddy and friend, and invited him and his wife to vacation with them that spring in the Bahamas. The mayor accepted, but took his girlfriend instead of his wife. The case wasn't pursued any further and got buried in the "unsolved crime" file at the police station.

The people that knew Larsen best weren't surprised at his reaction. He dealt with the pain, both physical and emotional, accepted it for what it was, and went on with his life. His father taught him that carrying grudges was dead weight on your back; that life sometimes wasn't fair or just, and was heavy enough all by itself. Larsen knew that he didn't want to deal with the burden of hauling around the dead weight of the past. He also knew that someday Dr. Baker would have to answer for all the wrongs of his life. In the meantime, he'd go on with his own.

CHAPTER 13

ESCAPE

Will looked nervously at Stanton, his confidence slipping, as the two boys squared off in the center of the mat. The rest of the class closed in a circle around them. Coach Barnes smiled through the whistle in his mouth and blew.

Stanton moved in aggressively, diving at his legs. Will put his hands up awkwardly to stop the attack, but before he knew what happened, was lying face down on the mat, Stanton riding him with his knee pressed into his spine. A hot pain shot from the base of Will's neck to his tailbone. Stanton lifted the knee, twisting Will's arm up and behind him like a police officer subduing a criminal. Will let out a primal and helpless moan that brought a roar of laughter from the spectators. Coach Barnes's smile stretched out over his long face. He was enjoying the show even more than the students. He blew his whistle again, stopping the action.

Baker released his grip, throwing Will's twisted arm to

the mat with a thud. The sound brought more laughter from the spectators. Will's face was red and he realized he was on the verge of tears. *Don't cry,* he thought.

Coach Barnes stepped on the mat, trying to hold back his laughter. He kneeled down to Will, still face down, and roughly picked him up off the mat. His smile faded as his voice once again boomed.

"Takedown, Baker," he said, and motioned for Will to take the "down" position on the mat. Will had seen wrestling matches at his old school and obliged by getting down on all fours in the center of the circle. He was already breathing heavily as Stanton mounted him, waiting for the next whistle.

Baker pressed his mouth close to Will's ear. "Your mom's a drunk," he whispered. "Is that why your dad left her? Is that why he blew his brains out?"

Coach Barnes blew the whistle and turned away from the action, slowly striding toward the locker room. He hated to miss the last act of the show, but wanted to be sure he couldn't be a witness against Stanton if he was asked.

Will didn't have time to think, and as the whistle blew he looked on as a spectator as his world moved in slow motion. He saw the laughing and contorted faces rooting on his nemesis, their shouts resonating through the gym like a muffled recording playing at half- speed. He swam underwater, struggling against the invisible current that whirled all around him. Again, before he had time to react, he was on the mat, this time looking up at the round fluorescent lights hovering from the high ceiling. He focused on the lights, trying to sap out some of their energy. Instead he felt Stanton's knee crashing into his crotch. The pain brought the world back into real time. The sounds and sights became hyper-focused. Stanton puffed his chest out and stood over him, proudly displaying his kill for the assembled audience.

Coach Barnes heard the cheers and laughter from the comfort of the padded chair in his office. He picked up his cell phone and dialed Dr. Baker. "You hear that?" he asked, pushing the phone toward the gym.

"Did he take care of the problem?"

The coach laughed. "I don't think Mr. Karras will be making any late night visits to your house anytime soon."

Dr. Baker's voice was without emotion. "Yeah, speaking of visits, I think I'll swing by the cemetery to see that boy's mother. She didn't show up for work again today. I might have to fire her unless she gives me a good reason to keep her," he said, hanging up without saying goodbye.

Without thought, Will tried to stand up, but the pain radiating from his groin forced him down to his knees. After a moment, he tried again. This time his legs didn't buckle and he ran for the door. Once in the hall, he turned right toward a door with a clouded and cracked "EXIT" sign above it, and pushed his way through it. He started running aimlessly, not noticing the frigid air or the pain coursing through his body from Stanton's cheap shot until he was a full block from the school.

CHAPTER 14

HOUSE CALL

M rs. Karras was sitting up on the couch in her still unfurnished living room when she heard the knock on the door. Her head pounded, but she had slept well the night before thanks to the sleeping pills. She was still dressed in her pajamas, her hair a knotty mess. She wearily walked to the door unaware of the time, but well aware that she should be at work. Slinking half-hunched toward the curtainless door, she saw her boss, Dr. Baker, waiting in the cold. Her heart sunk. He cupped his hands over the window and gawked inside. The pose highlighted his sharply angled eyebrows making him appear more evil and imposing than usual. Wiping the sleep from her eyes, she opened the door.

"Hello, Ellen," he said, his voice more than serious.

She was apologetic. "Dr. Baker. I'm sorry. I guess I must have overslept again. Please come in."

He stepped in the house, gazing judgmentally around the room, shaking his head in disgust.

"Please sit down," she said, directing him toward the plastic patio furniture in the kitchen.

He heard her, but stood his ground in front of the door, his face serious. "This isn't going to work," he said, his tone short and sharp.

"I..."

"Right. I know what you've been through, but you're not coming to work, you smell like a liquor store, and the times you are at work you're a zombie."

"I'm sorry," she said, running her fingers through her tangled hair.

His dark eyes flashed and he raised his voice. "I don't *need* sorry. What I *need* is someone to show up for work on time. I hired you as a favor to a friend of mine in Rochester. I knew it would be a mistake, and it has been a mistake, and I don't make mistakes or make it a habit to be around mistakes. You," he said poking his finger into her chest, "are a mistake that I don't need in my office. And your son is a mistake that doesn't *need* to be in our school or our town," he growled.

Her motherly instincts reappeared and took over. "My son has nothing to do with my problems. You leave him out of this." Her voice betrayed her, and lacked the authority she was hoping for.

He moved uncomfortably close. She could smell the stale coffee on his breath. "Your son is a vandalizing piece of white trash. He associates with trailer trash and he's lucky I didn't have him arrested Saturday night."

She didn't understand. Will had never been in trouble with the police. "What are you talking about?"

He turned from her and walked to the sink, gazing out the window at the headstones. "It's not important. I think he'll be getting what he deserves today at school."

She put her head down, her eyes welling with tears. "You leave Will out of this. I'm sorry. I'll be there tomorrow. This has all been rough on us." She barely managed to get the words out.

Dr. Baker's eyes softened, his lips rolling over in a sarcastic pout. He walked toward her and gently put his hands on her shoulders.

"Oh," he began mockingly, "Are you upset because your husband left you for another woman? I can't imagine why he did that. Look at you...you're such a fine catch all haggard and strung out on God knows what." His nose curled up in a snarl. "I can't believe anyone would leave you. You look great. I mean, you're carrying a bit of extra weight on you, but that's to be expected from a woman of your age." His hands wandered lower until he pinched the extra layer of skin around her waist. He moved his mouth close to her ear, his voice a whisper. "I like a woman with a little meat on her bones," he hissed, exchanging the pinch for a caress. "Why don't you do some work from home for me today?" he said, moving in to kiss her.

She was repulsed, and wanted to move away, but couldn't. She needed the job. Closing her eyes, she let him kiss her. His stale, hot breath left her paralyzed. Her lips were cold, limp, and unresponsive, but he continued anyway. She felt a sudden and slow tremble take control of her hands. It crawled up her arms, into her neck and head, until finally her entire body was shaking uncontrollably, every muscle rebelling against itself.

Dr. Baker stepped back in confusion. His face tightened as he watched her entire being battle with some unseen force. His face contorted in disgust. Ellen clenched her eyes shut tightly, her lids quivering in rhythm with the rest of her body.

She never saw it coming.

The doctor pivoted on his toe, utilizing his entire body weight into a textbook right cross. The blow landed solidly on her chin, and sent her crashing down to the floor where she lay motionless. Dr. Baker kicked her in the thigh until she came to. Her ears rang and her vision was blurred. She put her hand to her lip, pulled it away, and inspected the blood on her fingers. Instinctively, she pulled her knees to her chest, and wrapped her arms around them, her body heaving with each breath. She stayed in that position, wailing like a trapped and wounded animal.

Dr. Baker calmly turned and walked out the door and to his car. Before turning the key, he sat and listened to the cries from inside the house. They brought him back to the sounds of the tortured animals of his past. A satisfying grin cracked over his lips as he sat in the driveway. The grin turned into a smile and stayed that way as he replayed the scene in his mind on his way back to the office.

CHAPTER 15

FATE IS AN ACCIDENT

The day had turned from gloomy to gloomier, the constant gray blanket of clouds taking on a purplish hue. A storm was taking a breath, waiting to exhale a punishing combination of wind and snow. If Will looked up he would remember that the last time he saw the same dull colors it had snowed a total of eight feet over six days. He would have remembered being snowed in with his mom and dad in their house in Fairport, without the comforts of electricity or heat. He would have remembered how much he cherished that week huddled next to the fireplace listening to a battery-operated radio, his father reading by flashlight while his mother busied herself by cooking whatever food they had in the house over the fire. He would have remembered how good it felt to be trapped and wrapped in the security of his house and family.

But he never looked up.

Instead he ran, just ran, not really knowing where or

who he was running to. The pain in his oxygen-starved leg muscles occupied his mind, providing a good diversion from any thoughts of his wrestling match with Stanton.

Still running, dressed only in his shorts and t-shirt, he crossed State Street and made his way to the wealthy part of town on Cayuga Street. His emotions flashed from rage to self-pity to hopelessness. The sidewalks were covered in a hard pack of snow and ice as his weary legs carried him over a driveway where he unknowingly turned to cross the wide road.

The sight of the street triggered his mind, flipping the switch from off to on for the first time since leaving the school. He thought of a starving dog he had once seen scrambling across an interstate in Rochester, and how it dodged traffic to get to nowhere on the other side. Will wondered if it survived – if it *wanted* to survive, and if it did, why? *I'm no different than that dog*, he thought, reliving the recent months of his life as he jumped out into the street.

The white Chevy Suburban bearing down on him snapped his senses back to the present. With locked brakes, the car fought the icy road and swerved wildly in an attempt to miss him.

But it was too late.

The driver didn't even have time to blow the horn before the car softly landed its plastic bumper into Will's hip. The jolt sent him spinning to the ground, his world again falling into a slow motion dream. He saw the lifeless branches of the tall trees, the ground closing in on him, and finally the purple sky overhead as he came to rest face-up on the icy pavement. Then he closed his eyes, closing the blinds and shutting out the ensuing storm overhead.

Jacob Larsen unbuckled his seat belt and ran to the fallen boy. His heart was racing as he knelt down next to Will. Before he could reach for his cell phone to call for help, Will slowly opened his blue eyes. Some unseen magnetic force pulled their pale blue eyes together, each staring in bewilderment at the image before them. They were staring into a mirror, seeing someone familiar, a lost but unforgotten friend. Not breaking his stare, Will made his way up and onto his elbows.

"What are you doing here?" Will asked in a surprisingly steady and confident voice.

Mr. Larsen snapped out of his hypnotic stare and helped Will to his feet. He recognized the boy from their brief lunch encounter in Miss Brick's office. "Will? Are you OK?" he asked ignoring the bizarre question.

"I never saw you coming," Will said as he brushed the snow from his legs and shoulders.

"Yeah, you kind of surprised me, too. Come on. We've got to get you in the car and to the hospital."

The whole scene was surreal. It was more than the fact that he had nearly run over a teenager running in shorts and a t-shirt in the middle of winter. There was something more, some inexplicable mixture of emotions that swirled together from the moment he looked into Will's dazed eyes. He took him by the arm and led him to the passenger seat.

The heat pouring out of the vehicle's vents sent a welcoming blanket of warmth through his entire body, enveloping him a cocoon of comfort. He looked himself over as Larsen hurried around the front of the car. Other than a small scrape on his elbow and a sore hip, he knew he was fine. He was amazed at how calm he was after all he had been through since getting to school that morning. The man – he flashed back to the moment he opened his eyes and saw Larsen's shining back at his – offered a strange and inexplicable sense of security.

"You never answered my question," Mr. Larsen said, climbing into the SUV. "Are you OK?"

A smile broke across Will's face as he looked himself over again. "Yeah," he said with a hint of a laugh, "I'm fine."

They started driving down Cayuga Street, the first street Will had seen as he and his mother made their way into his new hometown. It seemed like years ago to him. He watched the brick mansions passing by once again, only this time he wasn't expectant and anxious about the town. He now knew what was in store for him: that it wasn't a place he wanted to be; that his classmates, with the exception of his small group of misfit friends, didn't want him there; that they had thrown more than just snowballs at him on Fall Street. The realization empowered him because at least now he knew who and what he was up against. He remembered overhearing an old Greek friend of his father's once saying through his strong accent, "It's better to live with the devil you know than the devil you don't know." At the time he didn't understand what the man meant. But now, remembering the feelings he first had when entering the village, he knew exactly what the man was talking about. He now knew the devil and could do something about it other than simply worry about him.

Larsen interrupted Will's thoughts. "Where do you live? I've got to talk to your mother." His voice was powerful, yet quiet. It carried a certain understated confidence that rendered respect without demanding it.

Will laughed again. "I'm really fine. The bumper barely hit me. I was more shocked than anything else. I've never been hit by a car before." That said, the two laughed together, their voices and breath oddly in sync with one another.

Will directed him toward the cemetery and painted a rough sketch of his story: that he had lived in Rochester and moved here when his mother got the job at the chiropractic college.

"How good would a garbage plate be right now?" he asked his passenger.

The question threw him, but his mood soared thinking about the food and his life a world away. "You know about Nick's?" he asked, closely tracing Larsen's profile against the shoddy houses whizzing past the driver's window. He felt like he already knew him.

Larsen laughed. "Yeah, that place helped clog a lot of my arteries when I was in college." He turned toward his passenger. "I went to St. John Fisher – spent about five years in Rochester.

"How did you know I'd know about Tahou's?"

Larsen smiled. "Angela – Miss Brick told me you were from Fairport. I just figured that any true-blooded teenager from around Rochester had to have had a plate some time."

The comfortable conversation gave Will the confidence to ask another question. "How did you end up here?"

"That's a long story. Maybe we can make homemade plates someday and I'll tell you all about it."

Will smiled at the thought of sharing a plate with the oddly familiar stranger. Suddenly, he remembered the first words he spoke to him after the accident: *What are you doing here?* Will chalked it up to just another piece of his recent life that just didn't make sense.

They turned left into the bumpy gravel driveway and Mr. Larsen rested the car, its engine still idling, in front of the house. Will saw his mother's car parked where it had been when he left for school earlier that morning. *She didn't go to work again*, he thought.

"No one's home."

"Will, I can't..."

Will looked Larsen in the eye, and caught a glimpse of himself reflecting from his eyes. "I'm fine." His voice was serious and reassuring. I was running home because I was late for a dentist appointment. That's why I didn't see you. My mom will kill me if I miss this appointment," he said.

Larsen was unconvinced; he knew that there was more to the story than that. But, he also knew that physically the boy appeared to be fine. He finally relented. "Okay," he said smiling at Will. "Give me her work number so I can call her."

Will jotted down a phony phone number, and walked to the shaky porch and into the house. Larsen looked at the number and shook his head. It wasn't even the right area code. He backed out and headed straight to Miss Brick's office to find out more about the boy, his mother, and their life.

CHAPTER 16

OBSTACLES

Ellen Karras was up and sitting in the kitchen sipping a glass of vodka at the plastic patio table when Will walked through the door. She needed the drink to help numb the pain in her face. Her lip was swollen and cut and her eyes were a puffy mixture of tears, Xanax, and alcohol. Her frazzled voice startled Will as he darted for the stairs.

"What are you doing home?" she asked.

Will jumped back. "I didn't see you there," he said, turning and taking her into view. He saw her lip, and moved in closer, a wide-eyed look of disbelief on his face. "What happened to you?"

She didn't respond to his question, her voice a tight and frayed rope straining to hold the weight of her life. "I asked you, what...are...you...doing...*home*?"

He tried to speak, but couldn't find his voice.

The rope finally gave way. "Damn-it, Will, why are you

here!" she exploded, slamming her hand on the table and sending the vodka glass airborne until it lay shattered on the floor.

Will inched his way backward and away from the woman he no longer knew, the whole time staring blankly at his mother's dark brown eyes, alive with fire. He still couldn't speak, think, or imagine what was happening to his world. Just when he thought his day could get no worse, that at least he made it to the safety of his house, his mother lashed out at him. Will needed to escape again. He shot out the door, and aimlessly ran deep into the sheltered serenity of the cemetery.

The sky stood still, purple, impatiently waiting to exhale the storm brewing inside it. He made his way down the gravel drive toward the back of the cemetery, his sanctuary from the madness that surrounded him. Once again he was at the spot where he had first spotted Isaac's shadow drifting through the stones. Bracing himself against the wrought-iron fence, his mind numb from the events of the young day, Will stared down the hill at the still brown waters of the canal. Everything – the trees, the water, his mother – was dead and without breath.

"You've had a rough one, huh?" The voice appeared out of nowhere, startling him. It was Isaac.

Will turned quickly, and when he recognized the shape standing just in front of him, his body relaxed. He was happy to see the sage stranger who knew so much about him and the world.

He closed his eyes, relieved. "Isaac," he said, "where did you come from? I didn't see you..."

The old man interrupted him, his voice calm, steady, and strong. "It's OK now, Will. I've been here all day waiting for you." Will tried to respond, but Isaac gently touched his hand to the boy's lips to quiet him. A peaceful wave of warmth rippled through Will's body. His cheeks flushed and Isaac softly withdrew his hand and turned around.

"Teddy Roosevelt," he said, as if speaking to the dead.

Will shifted his eyes, wondering if he was supposed to respond.

He finally did. "Okay," he said expectantly.

Isaac waited, still facing away from Will. "What do you know about him?" he finally asked.

Will searched the history file in his brain. "He was the president in the early 1900's?" he questioned, not confident in his answer.

Isaac spun around spryly and his eyes lit up. "Right! My own father saw him give a speech once when he was about your age. He worshiped that man; probably because he was a lot like Teddy himself. My father believed in hard work – work until you wear yourself too thin to remember your problems. He learned that from Roosevelt."

He glanced at the brewing sky and then back at Will. "Did you know that Roosevelt was a sickly boy? That he had asthma so bad that he couldn't catch his breath after walking up the stairs. That was when he was a boy! But he didn't give in. He knew the only way to beat his illness was to face it head on. He exercised the asthma out of his body by making up his mind that it wasn't going to stop him. He was a fighter. He fought for his sanity when his wife and mother died on the very same day! Can you imagine? He didn't let it rip him in half the way an ordinary man would. He went to North Dakota, a wild frontier in the 1880's, and worked his body to exhaustion to knock out the pain in his mind. It was the way my dad lived his life, how he taught me to live mine, and how I taught my son to live. You can't sit down and take life. You gotta take life *on*.

"'The boy who is going to make a great man must not make up his mind merely to overcome a thousand obstacles, but to win in spite of a thousand repulses and defeats.' Those were his words." He studied Will's face. "Do you get it? He might as well have been talking about you – hell, *to* you. You're that boy. You aren't going to be that 'great man' just making up your mind to do it. You've got to do it, got to overcome your obstacles and *win*.

"Yeah, you've got troubles. The man that raised you killed himself, your mom's sick, you're living in a damn cemetery, and some son of a bitch isn't letting you forget any of that. You can't do anything to bring back a dead man, but you might be able to do something for your mother, and you sure as hell can do something about that Baker boy. Make up your mind to do something. Then don't just do it for the sake of doing it. Do it to win." Isaac's voice suddenly flicked to a fiery whisper. "Do it to win."

Will didn't know what to say. There was so much to take in. He knew that what he had said was true, but was trying to figure out how this man seemed to know more about him than he knew about himself. The wind picked up and sent a chill through him. Suddenly aware of the cold, Will wrapped his arms around himself, grappling with the man's words. He looked up. The purple sky had cracked leaving a charcoal-streaked sea above.

He finally spoke. "You're talking about Stanton, but how did you know? And, how did you know about..."

"Don't do that, Will," Isaac interrupted gently. "What I know and how I know it will be clear soon enough, but that's not your concern right now. Trust yourself enough to trust me."

Isaac's face changed, the serious expression substituted with a warm smile. His eyes melted into Will's, and he reached out toward him. "You're cold," he said, cupping Will's face in both his hands. "Don't be cold. There's too much cold in the world today. That's not you. Let the world know that's not you."

A sudden and familiar warmth filled Will's face, and slowly moved through his neck, torso, and limbs until his whole body simmered with some unseen force leaking from Isaac's hands. The tepid temperature changed him. He was an old house: calm, solid, and settled firm on its foundation. The warmth drained from Isaac into Will, and the old man began trembling with cold.

A look of concern painted across Will's face. "Are you OK? You're so cold."

Isaac answered with a satisfying smile that started in his eyes and crept and washed down over his entire face. He looked at Will with a father's pride as a tear appeared and gently rolled down his cheek.

"Will!"

Will's head snapped toward the voice. It was Robert running toward him. He looked back toward Isaac, but he was gone, the snow around the fence revealing only his own footprints.

As Robert neared him, the sky exhaled and released its burden in a gasp of huge snowflakes blowing sideways in the wind.

CHAPTER 17

BRICKS

By the time Larsen made it to her office, Brick looked frazzled. The school day was over, and the stresses of the morning showed on her face. She closed the door behind him.

Without exchanging pleasantries, Larsen asked, "What do you know about a boy named Will Karras?"

Brick stopped shuffling papers from behind her desk and looked up at him, surprised, her eyebrows reaching for the faint lines in her forehead. "I can tell you that he's the reason I'm flipping out," she said, her voice melodically singing and emphasizing each syllable. She sat down, took a deep breath, and forced a smile to her lips.

Her concern brought a smile to Jacob's face. He respected her passion for her job and the kids. He sat down on the couch beside her desk expectantly waiting for the story to unfold.

"Stanton Baker..."

"Oh, God!" Larsen interrupted, rolling his eyes.

"Right, your favorite. Stanton Baker has been picking on Will like *crazy* ever since he got here. He's the latest victim. A couple of my girls told me about it, and I was going to talk to Will about it today, *but*," she paused for dramatic effect, and then told him about the incident in the gym.

Larsen shook his head in disgust. "He's from Rochester. What's his story? Why did they move here?"

She told him about the suicide, how Dr. Karras left the family penniless, and how Mrs. Karras moved here to get a job at the Chiropractic College.

He shook his head again, his face sincere with grief for Will and his mother, and then told her about the accident. "You know, Angela," he started after a moment, "There's something strange about Will Karras – some weird vibe I got from him. I can't put it into words, but I feel like I have some kind of connection with this kid. I want to help him." His face was grave, filled with an expression Miss Brick hadn't seen before. He looked like a child who'd lost something he'd never even had in the first place. Brick's eyes flashed to the photo of Larsen on her desk. She remembered what Robert said to Will about Larsen and him looking alike.

"I'm going to give you his folder," she said, pulling a bulging manila folder from a stack on her desk. "If anyone ever found out I let you look at it I'd be fired...like, in a second." The bold move took her by surprise. She never allowed teachers to take the student's cumulative folders out of her room let alone a friend take it out of the school.

"Pleeeeaaaaase," she pleaded, "please don't let anything happen to it or let anyone see you with it."

Jacob took the folder. His eyes told her how much he appreciated her trust. "I'll look at it right now."

She smiled at him. "No you won't," she said, playfully pushing him toward the door. "I've got a meeting in here with the 'The Mac' right now. I'm going to try to convince him not to suspend our Will for busting out of the school."

Jacob understood. "The Mac" was Mr. Macini. He ran a tight ship, and Larsen knew that Miss Brick really would lose her job if "The Chipmunk" saw him with a student's cumulative folder.

"Say no more," he said with a wink. He neatly tucked the file in his bulky ski jacket and walked out the door.

CHAPTER 18

REVELATIONS

T he chunky flakes stuck to the ground, bleaching the graveyard pure white. The sky that just a minute before was an ominous eye leering over the town was now hidden with the tide of snow pushing its way to the ground. Will, a lanky and scantily clad statue among the headstones stood dumbfounded in the center of it all.

Robert was still calling his name as he trudged toward him. Will could see the faint outline of Travis's truck behind the storm of snowflakes. Robert grabbed him by the arm.

"Come on, man! You're going to freeze to death out here!"

Will stared blankly at his friend. "Where's Isaac?" he asked.

"Who?"

"Isaac. He was just here. You had to see him. I was talking to him."

Robert raised his voice against the cold wind. The snow

was blowing sideways. "Come on, Will! You're alone. No one's here but the two of us and our stuttering friend in the truck." He pointed to where the truck should be, but the white out made it impossible to see it. Robert put his arm around Will and guided him toward the invisible truck. Travis seemingly appeared out of nowhere and wrapped his sweatshirt around Will's shoulders. The three boys pushed one another, Will first, into the truck through the driver's side door. Travis pulled the rusty door shut. Will snapped the heater blower off and gave Travis the sweatshirt.

"Are you c-c-c-crazy? Turn the f-f-freakin' heater back on," Travis snapped. Robert grabbed the sweatshirt off of Travis's lap and pushed it to Will.

"I'm not cold," said Will, throwing it back to Travis.

"Fine, I'll w-w-wear it. It's the only th-th-thing I've got since S-S-Saturday night."

"Shut up. I'll give you my freakin' jacket, you baby!" Robert lashed out. He turned toward Will and grabbed his arm. "He's probably got hypothermia and can't feel the cold." Puzzled, he put both hands on Will's arm, and then grabbed the other one. They were warm. He cupped Will's face in his hands. His face was warm, too. He looked at him in disbelief. "You're not cold. I was only outside for a minute and I'm freezing and you're..."

Annoyed, Will pushed his friend's hands from his face. "I told you I wasn't cold! I always turn warm when that old man touches me."

Travis was genuinely disturbed. "An old m-m-man t-t-touches you?"

"Not like that," Will hissed. "Didn't you guys see him? Isaac?"

Travis and Robert turned to each other. "Will, I told you, no one was out there with you. Not when we pulled up, not when I got out of the truck to get you, and not when I walked up to you."

Travis put the truck into first gear and eased the clutch out. He could barely see the path through the blowing and drifting snow, and slowly chewed through the snow-covered gravel toward Will's house.

"What happened today?" Robert asked.

Will wasn't sure what he was asking about.

"At school? With Stanton?"

"D-d-do y-y-you want t-to go to your house or…"

"Go to my house!" Robert ordered. Travis obliged and turned onto Bayard Street. He turned to Will. "So?"

Will told the boys everything that had happened – Stanton's beat down in the gym, nearly getting killed by Larsen, his mother's outburst – everything except Isaac. They didn't see him in the cemetery so he wasn't going to mention him again. Will wasn't going to risk driving away his only friends because they thought he was delusional.

"Did they let school out early?" The day's events made him lose all sense of time.

Robert laughed. "Will, school got out half an hour ago. Alex told me he saw you running across the street in your gym clothes so I grabbed Travis and we bolted right after school. We figured you'd be in the cemetery when you weren't at your house."

Travis turned up Ovid Street, his truck one of the few vehicles braving the blizzard. "Are y-y-you going b-b-back to school tomorrow?"

"Yeah," he answered quietly. "I've got to figure out how I'm going to take care of some things; and then I'm going to take care of them."

Surprisingly, Larsen's flight from Rochester that night wasn't cancelled. Most of the storm swept south of the airport, and the plane would only be delayed half an hour. Although he did as much work as he could from home, he needed to be in New York City the next morning for a meeting with a publisher.

The Greater Rochester International Airport wasn't crowded. It was small and convenient and got its "International" moniker for the two 30-minute flights to Toronto it offered. Larsen sat uncomfortably in one of a line of seats that gave him a clear view of his plane and the weather outside.

He pulled Will's file from his briefcase. It was bulging with papers from Will's elementary and middle school history in Fairport. Colors flashed in front of him as he began thumbing through it. Each section was coded with a different hue – green for photos, yellow for testing, white for personal information – to distinguish it from the next. He stopped at the green "photos" section.

The collection of pictures showed Will from kindergarten

all the way to the ninth grade. Larsen studied them all carefully, but was drawn to the first in the series – the kindergarten photo. His mind wandered as he stared at the four-year-old boy, innocent, his whole life ahead of him. It reminded him of a photo of him at that age. The bright blue eyes, sandy blonde hair, and toothy smile revealed an excited anticipation of some great and unknown event yet to happen. He stared at it, lost in the memories of his own childhood.

"Ladies and gentlemen, US Airways flight 422 with nonstop service to New York LaGuardia will begin boarding at this time," a woman's raspy voice called out over the intercom. The announcement startled him. He carefully shuffled the papers back into the folder and into his bag, and got in line.

The plane took off on time bringing with it a short and uneventful flight. By the time he made it to his hotel in Manhattan, it was past 11:00. Restless and surprisingly awake, he decided to take another look at Will's cumulative folder. As he lifted it to his lap, a faded and wrinkled paper, embossed with the official New York State seal, fell onto the bed. It was Will's birth record:

STATE OF NEW YORK CERTIFICATE OF LIVE BIRTH
OFFICE OF VITAL STATISTICS
CERTIFIED COPY

This is a certification of name and birth facts
on file in the Bureau of Vital Records,
Department of Health, City of Rochester, NY

Date of Birth: __10/1/92__

Time of Birth: __7:14 AM__

Certificate Number: __327-453-8771__

Place of Birth: __Highland Hospital, Rochester, NY__

Full Name of Child: __William Isaac Larsen__

Sex: __Male__

Mother's Name: __Sarah Battaglia__

Father's Name: __Jacob Larsen__

CERTIFIED BY

Earline Price

City Registrar, Rochester, NY

CHAPTER 19

IN SPITE OF A THOUSAND DEFEATS

W
ill was worried about his mother, but had no idea what a teenage boy could do for a grown woman suffering with horrible depression. *Depression*, he thought as Travis pulled into Robert's driveway. He was sure of that diagnosis, but didn't want to be sure of the drinking and drugs that had snuck up and into her life. He had watched her metamorphosis and feared she was sure to drown in her addiction if he didn't do something for her.

But he would have to deal with that later. There was nothing he could do for her tonight. Robert's mother again treated the boys to a large take-out pizza from the Venice. Travis left just after 10:00, and Robert and Will retired to the bedroom.

"You haven't asked me anything else about Stanton."

Robert pulled a faded Metallica shirt over his head and peeled the covers back on the bed. "If there's one thing I learned from all the crap I've been through," he said crawling into bed, "it's not to ask someone with a lot on their mind a bunch of questions. I used to hate that. I already asked you what happened today with that idiot. You told me what you wanted to tell me, and I figure you'll tell me more when you're ready to talk about it." He turned on his side and looked at Will on the floor in a sleeping bag. "Between Stanton beating you, Larsen running you over, and your mother flipping out on you, I can't imagine what's going through your head."

Will smiled. "Thanks."

"No problem."

A moment passed. "I'm going after him tomorrow."

"I knew that's what you had in mind," Robert said, unfazed by his declaration.

"Why did you think that?"

"I could see it in your eyes. And also what you said in the truck. You sounded real sure of yourself even if you weren't sure what you were going to do. I don't know if that made any sense."

Will laughed at his friend's perception. "Yeah, that made a lot of sense."

"Just so you know, I've never seen anyone beat him up."

"There's always a first time," Will whispered to himself.

The snow outside had subsided, and by the time the alarm beeped the next morning, the sun was shining. Will was restless as Robert's mother drove them to school. Isaac never said Roosevelt didn't get nervous. He shifted uncomfortably in the cramped back seat, a thin film of sweat forming on his forehead. The ride went by quickly, and the two climbed out of the car and walked into the warmth of the lobby.

Alex was standing in the corner, alone, and met the boys just inside the door. "The Chipmunk's looking for you, Will. He asked me if I'd seen you yet this morning. You're probably going to get detention for skipping out yesterday."

"Good morning to you, too," Robert answered sarcastically.

"Will!" a voice rang out from across the crowded room. It was Stanton.

The voice sent Will's heart racing, and now the dam that held back all the things he hadn't thought about gave way, sending anxiety, fear, and panic pouring through his body. He felt his hands getting clammy and his knees begin to shake. His brain was in fight or flight mode, but unlike yesterday, Will was set on the fight today.

"Will!" Another voice rang out from just in front of the doorway. He turned, and there, standing in the corner illuminated by some faint rays of sunshine peeking in, stood Isaac. He was dressed in the same suit and fedora he always wore. Will squinted toward the figure. Isaac smiled and nodded approvingly, his eyes, sharp and serious, sent him a message: *Now is the time.*

The nod sent the fear and panic back into its cave faster than it had been unleashed. Isaac's appearance transmitted warmth, calm, and peace through the air, and splashed it over him. He was focused and unafraid. *Now is the time,* he thought confidently.

Stanton strode toward him. "Hey, Will." The bully was

intentionally calling attention to himself. But the assembled audience wasn't large enough for him yet.

"Hey, hey, hey, hey!" he said, waving his arms to hush the crowded lobby. The room grew eerily quiet as more eyes descended upon him. The stage was his. "Hey, Will! Aren't you a little overdressed today?" he hissed, pushing people aside to get to his victim.

His joke was greeted with a dull blanket of laughter. It was a small school, and by now nearly everyone had heard about Will's escape from the gym. Every eye in the lobby was on Stanton. He seized the attention like an actor in a one-man show.

He stood a few feet away from Will. "You forgot your gym shorts. It's a great day for a run." More laughter filled the room. "No, no, no, no," he said, quieting his audience and inching closer to Will. "I'm sure his mom warmed him up when he got home with a nice hot bowl of vodka!"

Stanton was now standing face to face with Will. His face was dark and brooding, while his tense body readied itself to deliver the first blow.

"Get lost, Stanton," Robert said in a low and even tone. In a flash, Stanton stabbed a leg behind Robert's heel, grabbed him by the shirt, and threw him to the ground. Two of Stanton's friends dragged him to a nearby wall to keep him from interfering again.

Stanton refocused his attention on Will. His voice boomed, vindictive, vengeful, and evil. "If the vodka didn't work, I know his father could have warmed him up with a nice hot piece of lead served up from his nine-millimeter."

The crowd gasped in a mixture of laughter, outrage, and horror; but Will didn't hear them. A quiet fire built within him. It lit the fuse. It bent his knees. It clenched his fist into a tight ball held chest-high. It braced his elbow against his hip. It exploded.

Will's legs unleashed all of their energy upward, sending his fist and the momentum of his entire body rocketing skyward and into Stanton's jaw. It was a textbook uppercut from a textbook he had never read. Stanton's jaw snapped shut, shattering at its hinge. His neck whipped his head back and his knees buckled. He lay, lights out, in a twisted heap on the floor at Will's feet.

The two thugs tending to Robert rushed over and tried to bring Stanton to his feet. He was conscious again, but his limp legs betrayed him and he fell back to the floor. Will felt someone tugging on his jacket. "Big Mac" had him by the arm and was pulling him through the stunned throng of students. They knew about Stanton's black belt, and couldn't believe that the lanky new kid had just leveled him. Some were laughing, others looked on angrily, and the rest stood with gaping mouths, shocked by what they had just witnessed.

The room was a chaotic blur to Will as he twisted his head around in an effort to catch a glimpse of Isaac. But there was no sign of him. The corner was empty except for the bright ray of sunshine that fell over the old man just a moment ago.

Will's body was limp, plodding along beside Mr. Macini as he dragged him past the gawking secretaries and into his office. He sat him down roughly in a hard-backed chair, plopped himself down behind his desk, and began ranting. Will didn't hear his words, just tiny echoes floating through the room, landing softly around his ears, and drowned out by the thoughts throbbing in his head.

"Are you listening to me? Answer me, young man!"

"Yeah," he said wearily.

Unsatisfied, he tapped his pen in rhythm with his words. "You *will* be suspended for five days for fighting. We don't tolerate fighting here at Mynderse." He paused. "Your suspension starts immediately. I'll call your mother."

He pointed to the door. Miss Brick, called by one of the secretaries, was waiting for him. She couldn't mask the pride in her eyes. It was just what he needed to see.

CHAPTER 20

THE RING

A receptionist from the Chiropractic College gave Mr. Macini the news: "Mrs. Karras no longer works with us," she said flatly. Next, "Big Mac" tried Will's home phone, but the number had been disconnected. Miss Brick would have to take him home.

Once out of the building, she put her arm around him. "I knew I should have checked up on you this morning," she said, admonishing herself aloud.

Will put his head down and chuckled. "There's nothing you could have done." He lifted his head looking straight ahead at the snow-covered soccer field. "I had to do it."

She understood, and although she'd only admit it behind closed doors to Larsen, she was glad he had done it. Stanton had been exploiting any weakness he could find in the other students for years without punishment. His intelligence and charm had convinced most his teachers and the administrators that he wasn't capable of such abuse.

Those who did suspect him were either friends with or afraid of his sadistic father.

The sky was dreary again, the sun having lost its battle with the matted gray clouds beneath it. They drove in silence down Cayuga Street, passing the site of the accident the day before. Will thought about Larsen, the man with the familiar blue eyes who had nearly killed him. He wanted to know more about him.

He squinted and looked at Miss Brick behind the wheel. "Is that Mr. Larsen your boyfriend?" he questioned with the curiosity and courage of a second-grader who didn't know better than not to ask.

She turned toward him quizzically, her shocked face meeting his. "What?" Her voice smiled with her face.

Will laughed at her reaction. He could tell he hit a nerve with her and boldly went on. "I saw the way you reacted the first day of school when Robert told me he was your boyfriend. And," he paused, checking her for any reaction, "I've seen you two at school hanging around each other." His voice was innocent and playful.

"Why are you asking me that?" she squeaked, embarrassed, and stopped at the light near Filthy's. She took her hands off the wheel and moved her long blonde hair over her ear. Her cheeks flushed red.

"Will," her head bobbed as she tried but failed to erase her smile. It was time to play the part of counselor. "Okay, you just beat a kid up and got suspended from school. Why are you asking me about him?"

The light turned green, and she lurched the car forward

toward the bridge. Will turned his head and looked at the empty canal. His voice turned serious. "He just seems like a good guy," he said.

She waited a moment to see if he was going to mention his encounter with Mr. Larsen the day before. Her intuition told her not to let him know she knew about it. When he didn't offer anything else, she began.

"He *is* a good guy," she said sentimentally. "He's a *great* guy," she added. They turned down Bayard Street. "But to answer your question, he's just a friend."

Will nodded and stared at the fresh snow blanketing the village. The magnitude of what had just happened at school really hadn't hit him yet. He knew he was suspended, but that didn't bother him. None of it bothered him right now because none of it seemed real. Everything was like a bad reality show where the producers throw an unsuspecting dolt into an impossible situation. It would be entertaining to watch, but not to be the star. The next scene would be him dealing with his mother.

She pulled the car into the cemetery and parked next to the house. Even though she had been Mynderse's counselor for six years, she never got used to seeing how some of her kids were raised or where they lived. Will was the first student she had that actually lived in a graveyard, and it saddened her. "I have to talk to your mother," she said in her official school voice. "I've got to make sure you're with an adult or I can't drop you off."

The door was unlocked, and Will led her into the dark and eerily quiet living room. It took a moment for each of their snow-blind eyes to adjust.

"I guess she's not here," he lied. The last thing Will needed today was to have the school counselor find his mom passed out drunk on the floor.

The floor creaked, breaking the silence. Mrs. Karras's shadow materialized in the bedroom doorway like a Polaroid print, slowly developing and revealing her blurry features and lines. Miss Brick was shocked. At first glance she only saw the deep caves that hid the woman's invisible eyes, and then slowly, as she stepped closer, the sagging and lifeless skin behind an expressionless mask came into focus.

Will didn't recognize the woman in front of him as his mother. She looked worse than he'd ever seen her. All three stood, momentarily frozen, staring at each other.

His mother took a step toward them, the floor again groaning under her weight. She growled at Will with a low, even, emotionless tone, her lips barely moving. "What are you doing home?"

Miss Brick answered for him, reluctantly moving closer with an extended hand. "I'm Angela Brick, the guidance counselor at Mynderse," she said in the most cheerful voice she could produce.

"Don't come any closer to me!" she exploded.

The force of the words stopped Miss Brick in her tracks. She pulled her hand back, and could feel her racing heartbeat throbbing in her neck.

"Mrs. Karras," she began calmly, "I just needed to be sure someone was home when I dropped Will off..."

"I asked you why you were home," she hissed, ignoring the stranger in her house.

"Will got..."

"I don't need you to speak for him."

Will felt his lips and teeth tighten against each other. A wave of sadness, anger, and embarrassment spilled over him. "I got in a fight at school, Mom," he said quietly.

"He got suspended from school for fighting..."

"I told you...not...to...speak for him!" Each word built to a final crushing crescendo. She reached for the Karras family photo sitting atop one of the cardboard boxes. With a quick flick she *Frisbee* threw it toward Miss Brick. The counselor ducked just in time, and the smiling family from another time smashed against the wall.

"Come on, Will!" Miss Brick urged. She grabbed him by the arm and pulled him toward the door. Will stumbled clumsily behind her, then wrenched his arm free. "Will, come on!" she said grabbing him again.

He shrugged his arm from Miss Brick's hand, turned around, and faced his mother. She was living death. Her eyes were still invisible, her skin gray and ashen. Her hair hung thin and straight over her shoulders and her frail body seemed twisted and contorted. Will's sad eyes begged the question – *Why?*

She laughed at the pathetic look on his face and stepped close to him. Her neck strained forward so that her lips were within inches of his face. "I should have never adopted you! Get out! You're not my son! Get out and don't come back!" The words shot out of her and landed like a bullet in the head.

He didn't feel the blast of cold, Miss Brick's fingers

digging into his arm, his legs folding underneath him, his face bouncing off the ice on the front porch, or the warm blood dripping out of his mouth. He didn't feel him pick himself up, spin away from Miss Brick, or run behind his house and into the dense and dead thicket of the gully below the cemetery.

Will and his world were numb.

Miss Brick tried to run after him, but the gully, nearly impenetrable, was deep and filled with thorny thatches of briar, the only surviving vegetation of the long Upstate New York winter. He quickly vanished from her sight as he moved deeper into the brittle brush. A thick spine ripped through his jacket and deep into his arm, sending a sharp bolt of pain through his body. His senses snapped back to life. He ripped the thorn from his arm and fell to the ground, a beaten soldier on a broken and battered battlefield.

Tears ran down his cheeks as he sat sobbing, contemplating his mother's words. Adopted. He was *adopted*?

"Mind if I sit down?"

Will snapped his neck around to the sound behind him. It was Isaac, dressed in his familiar uniform, standing comfortably in a row of thorns.

Will caught his breath between sobs. "Watch out for the pricker bushes," he said. "They're everywhere."

"Those won't hurt me," he replied. He let out a grunt and sat down next to Will. The woods were silent.

Will took stock of his position for the first time since sitting down. They were far into the woods, his house well out of sight. He realized that there was no way to reach the spot from the cemetery without descending the steep hills on both sides of them. From every angle they were invisible to the world.

"How did you get down here?" Will asked, trying to regain his composure. The sight of his trusted friend helped calm him down.

Isaac huffed. "Will," he paused, "there are things you need to know. Things you're ready to know."

Will reached for his lip and smudged the blood into the snow, staining away its purity. He fixed his gaze on his arm. Another drop of blood trickled onto his jacket.

Isaac began. "It's about time you know the truth. My name was Isaac Larsen. I was born in 1920 in Oil City, Pennsylvania. I was a first generation American - my parents came here from Norway in 1900." His voice was friendly and familiar, and sounded more like he was telling a story in front of a warm fireplace rather than in a cemetery gully in the dead of winter. "We didn't have much growing up, but we had what we needed. My folks didn't have any education, but they knew that I would. They insisted on it. I had to quit school in the seventh grade when my father died, and take a job on a barge running oil down to Pittsburgh. I worked the third shift – that's night work – and finally went back to school during the days when I was 16. Earned my high school diploma."

He looked up at the gray sky for a moment, and then into Will's eyes. "In 1942, just after Pearl Harbor, I joined the Marines. I did my basic training on Parris Island, and ended up in Egypt for the North African invasion." Lost in the memory, his eyes again drifted to the sky. "When I got back to the States I went back to work on the river and married the love of my life. She was beautiful and a bit younger than me," he added with a wink. "Eventually, I earned my Associate's Degree from the community college up in Jamestown. That degree got me promoted, off the barge, and into the office – I was in charge of 22 men," he said proudly. He turned his head away toward the tall trees lining the hill. "In 1965 we had our first and only child, a boy, Jacob." He paused, letting the full effect of his words work on the boy.

Will stared into Isaac's eyes, his face a picture of confusion. "Mr. Larsen," he said, matching Isaac's subdued voice. "He's your son?"

Isaac nodded, his face bright with a father's pride. "He's my son."

"I don't really know him," Will confessed, "but...I kinda *feel* like I know him."

Isaac's face turned gravely serious. "You know him."

The sun broke through the wallpaper-gray sky, shining a spotlight of sun directly over Isaac's face. The two sat quietly, both lost in their thoughts until Isaac finally broke the silence. "Will," he began, "I won't be seeing you anymore – at least not for quite a long time." His voice carried a subdued strength. The spotlight still hovered and shined on him; the moment was his. "I've got to go back to my wife...to the people I need, and, more importantly, who need me."

An alarming look of sadness washed across Will's face. "But *I* need you," he blurted out.

"I know you need me, but there are others who need you more: Mrs. Karras, Miss Brick, and most importantly, Jacob."

Will shook his head, dumbfounded. "I don't understand."

"I know you don't," Isaac said softly, "but you will. You will understand." He reached into his chest pocket and pulled out a ring. Holding it between his thumb and forefinger, he lifted his head, lowered his eyes to it, and slowly stretched his arm forward toward Will. It was a platinum engagement ring with one modest diamond gently set in its center. The sun-spotlight caught it, brilliantly and blindingly illuminating the stone. Will squinted, and Isaac sighed and smiled. "This ring is for you. I was told to give it to you so you could deliver it back to the hands from which it came. She told me to tell you that she will always be with you, and to give the person you're delivering it to a message." Will started to talk, but the old man interrupted. "Don't worry, you'll know who that person is when the time is right." Isaac's satisfying smile grew wider, and he delicately placed the ring in Will's hand. Will looked at it, his heart racing. It was the most beautiful thing he'd ever seen. Isaac took both his hands and cupped them over Will's and the ring. Warmth sparked from the ring and again filled Will. This time, though, Isaac didn't shiver. The two were one, basking in the comfort of the ring and each other.

Isaac paused to take a deep and rattling breath. "She told me to make sure you tell him that brick is always the best foundation for a home."

Will closed his eyes and thought to himself, *What is this?*

Isaac's response was like a feather. "It's love."

When Will opened his eyes, Isaac was gone, leaving only the bright sunbeam where he had stood. He knew he would never be alone again.

CHAPTER 21

HOMECOMING

Isaac's glow rested on Will's shoulders, filling him with a fresh sense of security and peace. The feeling cleansed his thoughts and helped sharpen the image of his life that had become so blurred. The ring was the last piece of his young life's puzzle, and he wasn't sure he'd ever be able to find out where it fit.

He began pushing his way back toward his house. As the tangled turf of briar bushes grabbed and clawed at his jacket and jeans, he remembered the one word that had sent him running out and into the gully in the first place: adopted. He was adopted. He felt the word, without reaction, sink like a heavy leaf in a pond, finally silently landing at the base of his soul. Adopted. Without fear, anxiety, or anger he contemplated the idea.

The intermittent glow of red, orange, and blue lights interrupted his thoughts as he made his way through the last of the brush and into the small field behind his house. An ambulance and two police cars were parked in his driveway. He quickened his pace and unconsciously slid the ring he'd been clutching since Isaac gave it to him over his pinky. Two EMT's were wheeling his mother out on a stretcher as he neared the porch. An officer grabbed him from behind and pushed him out of the paramedics' way.

"You don't need to be here, son," he said with authority. "You need to go home."

Will turned to him, startled. "That's my mom," he said, his voice solid and unfaltering. He flailed his arms to get out of the officer's grip. "What's the matter with her?"

The cop grabbed him again, more gingerly this time, and spun Will toward him. "Just step aside and let the EMT's get her in the ambulance..."

Will shrugged him aside again and ran to the stretcher. The paramedics were struggling to push it through the snow. He walked with them toward the ambulance. His mother's face was gray, her lips blue beneath the oxygen mask over her mouth. He grabbed her hand. It was as cold as the late winter air.

"Come on now, son," the cop's voice was softer now. He gently pulled Will toward him. "I'll drive you to the hospital. Just let them do their jobs. They're trying to save your mother's life."

The nearest hospital was in Geneva, a 20-minute drive from Seneca Falls. Will and Officer Barasso led the way, speeding and clearing a way for the ambulance close behind. The scenery, pure and undisturbed yesterday but salt and dirt stained today, spun past them in a whirlwind.

The chubby officer momentarily took his eyes off the road to look at Will. "Your mom's lucky we showed up when we did," he said.

Will looked him in the eye then shifted his attention to the man's portly stomach rubbing against the steering wheel. "Did she call you?" he asked quietly.

"Oh no," the officer answered assuredly. "Dr. Baker called us to come get you." He paused, waiting for Will's reaction.

Will met the cop's eyes, stunned. His heart skipped a beat. "Why?" he asked, and then, remembering the morning that seemed like years ago, answered his own question. "The fight."

"The fight," the officer nodded. "He wants to press charges against you for knocking his son out," he chuckled. Officer Barasso knew Stanton, and didn't like him. He was the lead detective for the Starlite Motel fire a few years back, and had fingerprints as well as other proof that the Baker boy had set the blaze. Just as he was about to bring the evidence to the District Attorney, the mayor inexplicably took him off the case. "If you want to keep your job," he told Barasso, "I'd forget anything about that motel fire." But the officer faithfully decided to go ahead with the investigation. When he brought the D.A. to the evidence room the next day, everything related to the case was missing. Within a month, he was demoted back down to patrol officer.

They were nearing the hospital, the town's large and closely spaced houses buzzing by. Will stared at them, lost in a web of thoughts. He finally shook his head in disbelief. Reading the officer's cues, he spoke up. "If I have to go to jail for knocking someone out, I'm glad it was Stanton Baker."

"You know what, Will? I'd go to jail just for the chance to see you knock him out again."

They turned into the hospital and up to the emergency entrance. Will got out of the car and watched as a team of doctors and nurses rushed his mother out of the ambulance and into the building.

CHAPTER 22

COWARDS

S itting in the hospital's small and sterile waiting room, Will slowly twisted Isaac's ring around his finger, staring at its unassuming beauty. It was modest and unpretentious. He didn't know anything about jewelry, but knew that this would be the kind of ring he would want to give to his own wife one day. It didn't scream for attention, but gave off an air of humble confidence.

"Will!" He recognized the voice as Miss Brick's before he looked at her. "Are you all right?" she asked, hugging him as he sat in his chair.

When she unclenched from him, Will saw Mr. Larsen standing directly behind her. They had come together.

"Hi, Will," he said, pressing his lips together in a respectful and sympathetic smile.

It had been more than an hour since his mother had been whisked away into the examining room. Doctors and nurses rushed in and out, but no one said a word to him about her condition.

The couple sat down on each side of him, and a moment later the door opened and Mrs. Karras was wheeled out past them and down the hall. There was no sense of urgency from the orderly pushing the gurney. Will stood up and looked at her face. Some of her color had returned, but she was still unconscious with a breathing tube now poking from her mouth.

A young, exhausted-looking doctor met them in the hall. "She's stable for now," he said. "We pumped twelve Xanax tablets out of her stomach. Clinically speaking, she was dead when she got here. We're moving her into a private room. You can go see her if you want, but she'll be probably be asleep for quite awhile." He paused and put his hand on Will's shoulder. "I've got to get back to the ER."

Will took a deep breath and stared at the faded square tiles on the floor. *Suicide...again*, he thought. The idea of the selfishness of the act sat heavily on him. Dr. Karras solved his problem with it and created more for his mother – more than she could handle. Problems she tried to solve in the same selfish way. Anger slowly crawled over him. "Cowards." The word, barely audible, escaped his mind and lips before he could stop it.

Miss Brick and Mr. Larsen heard him, but didn't respond. She shared a pitiful look with Larsen and instinctively put her arm around Will, holding him close to her.

The doctor, nearing the entrance to the ER door, stopped in his tracks and turned back to them. "Oh yeah," he said as if he'd forgotten something important. The three looked up in unison, watching as he made his way to them. "Who is Isaac?" he asked. "She kept mentioning 'Isaac.'"

Will and Larsen's heads snapped toward each other, a look of shock and confusion painted on their faces. The doctor stood in front of them waiting for an answer. When it didn't come he laughed and shook his head. "I'm sorry," he apologized, "It was probably nothing...just the drugs. I thought one of you might be Isaac."

Miss Brick spoke up. "No," she answered for the three of them. "None of us are Isaac. Do you know an Isaac?" she asked, looking at both of them. Larsen and Will, frozen in shock, both shook their heads. The doctor apologized again and made his way back down the hall.

By the time Miss Brick remembered that Larsen's father's name was Isaac she knew not to ask. There was something in both of their faces that told her that his name was best left unmentioned for the time being.

CHAPTER 23

A GHOST IS BORN

Will decided not to go in to see his mother. He was angry, and had seen enough of her lying unconscious at home since they'd moved to Seneca Falls. Larsen invited him out to get something to eat and Miss Brick volunteered to stay at the hospital.

Will climbed back into the SUV that had nearly run him over the day before. Except for the classic rock station quietly churning in the background, the ride was quiet. Neither wanted to talk. Will was numb from the avalanche of events from the day, while Larsen was trying to figure out how he was going to tell Will all he had to share with him.

The drive went by in a blur, and before Will realized it they were stepping inside The Deluxe, an historic home turned Italian restaurant. A pudgy middle-aged Italian woman with big, dark hair seated them at a table near the back. Since it was mid-afternoon, the restaurant was nearly deserted, the only other customers a family of six on the other side of the large room. Will watched the satisfied father, listening contentedly to his children's conversation with a proud smile on his face. Will envied the scene.

Mr. Larsen broke the silence at their table. "Get whatever you want, Will," he said nervously with a forced grin.

"I'm really not that hungry." He was still looking at the family across the room.

With all the effort of jumping into a freezing-cold pool of water, Mr. Larsen dove into his story. "When I was in my senior year of college in Rochester, I thought I had everything: good grades, a lot of close friends, and most importantly, the woman I was going to marry." The abrupt beginning gave Larsen Will's full attention. He stared into his eyes, again feeling as if he was looking into a mirror. Larsen went on. "I had everything that I didn't have when I was growing up. Things weren't really great for me in high school. My mom died when I was your age – she was in a car accident. We were close, and after that things kind of fell apart for me. I drew into myself – didn't want to hang out with my closest friends anymore. Eventually I started running around with some not-so- great kids."

He turned away from Will, shaking his head and laughing at the same time. "I kind of turned into a loser, and I guess by the time I was in about eleventh grade I was smoking pot every day before school and drinking a lot. I even got arrested twice in high school. Once for stealing a case of beer from a convenience store and once for getting busted with a bag of weed on me at school." He hesitated long enough to take a sip of water to help cure his shaking voice.

"Fortunately, and unbelievably, through all of that I managed to keep my grades up – straight A's. It's weird, but I still didn't want to disappoint my dad...or my mom. I always felt like she was watching me, and both my parents had successfully brainwashed me into believing that my grades were the winning ticket to success and happiness – especially my father. He was something – quiet, smart, and tough." He laughed softly. "He never raised a hand to me, but he should have – and could have done some damage. He was the middleweight boxing champion in his Marine regiment. Dad never talked about it, but his old war buddies always said that he had an uppercut that could take a man's head off.

"By the time I was a senior, I was partying every day after school. My new friends called me the 'stoned Einstein' because I was still making great grades and even got a scholarship to a little four-year private college in Rochester – you know, St. John Fisher. The guys I was hanging out with were going to work on the barges or in the factories just like their parents. It was hard to leave them behind because I knew that they'd spend their lives in Oil City and end up getting buried there, too."

He took a deep breath and noisily blew it out. "I partied like crazy my first semester of college, and for the first time in my life I failed a class – actually three – of the five I was taking. I was put on 'academic probation,' which didn't really bother me. I started not caring. When I got home for Christmas vacation I could see how much my bad grades and behavior were eating my father up inside. He tried to talk to me, but I just didn't care. I didn't want to hear about education being 'the key to my future,' or about how he didn't have the opportunities that I was throwing away. To me, the partying was more important than anything else, and I figured I'd go out with a bang during the spring semester, and then go to work with my old buddies in Pennsylvania." A roar of laughter from the other table sent Larsen's gaze to them. He looked satisfyingly at the family sitting across the room.

"But," he raised his voice playfully, his spirits obviously lifted by the sounds across the room and the subject he was about to bring up. "But, I was saved!" Will's expression changed. While his parents had dragged him to the local church most of his life, he didn't consider himself a religious person. Larsen picked up on the look on his face and laughed. "No, not like that," he said with a smile. "No, my saving grace was a girl named Sarah."

Larsen's spirits lifted with the sound of her name. His eyes softened and set the tone for the rest of his face. "She was beautiful, inside and out. We met in one of my English classes, hit it off right away, and went out on our first date a week after meeting. I took her to Tahou's for a garbage plate," he said with a chuckle.

Will looked at him in admiration. Mr. Larsen was real. He was opening up to him like no adult had done before. He was the antidote to all the grown-ups he'd known in his life who pretended to be something they weren't – like his own parents.

Larsen continued his story, his eyes a million miles away. "Almost immediately I put away the drugs and picked up the books. She was a smart girl and I wanted her to know how smart I was, too. I didn't need to party anymore. I had found something way better than drugs." He paused and asked the waitress to refill his nearly empty glass of water. "We dated until we were seniors in college."

He stopped, his expression heavy with the weight of the memory he was about to share. "That's when we found out she was pregnant." The party at the other table got up and left the dining room, leaving an eerie quiet in their wake.

"As soon as I found out, I asked her to marry me. I gave her a ring – it wasn't much – but it was all I could afford, and we got engaged. We only had one semester of school left and I knew she was the woman I wanted to spend the rest of my life with. I knew that without her I would have ended up with my old friends drinking and working the rest of my life away on a barge or in a factory." His lips anxiously twisted before finally blurting it out. "The baby...my son...that was you."

Will's forehead and eyes wrinkled in confusion and uncertainty. He couldn't speak, and even if he could, he wouldn't know what to say. Larsen smiled broadly and a tear rolled from his eye.

Will shook his head. The revelation of his mother's words earlier that day rushed back to the front of his mind. She said he was adopted. He didn't know what to make of it at the time, but now he knew it was true. The people he knew to be his parents his whole life weren't. Mr. Larsen, the man who he felt so inexplicably connected, the man with his eyes, was his real father.

Larsen reached into his jacket pocket and unfolded the copy of the birth certificate. Will stared at it, absorbing every detail of the faded paper.

"What happened to Sarah...I mean, my...*mom*?" he asked, shocked by his own words.

Larsen stared at the ceiling, struggling against the memory. He refocused his eyes on the glass of water in front of him. "It was strange because she didn't have any problems the whole time she was pregnant with you. Everything was fine. But something went wrong when she went into labor. She started bleeding and the doctors couldn't stop it. They gave her blood transfusions – tried everything they could. She died that night a few hours after you were born."

The waitress came over to get their order, but left when neither one of them acknowledged her. Will sat in stunned silence, turning his attention to the empty plate on the table. "Why did you give me up?" he finally asked soberly without looking up.

"When Sarah – your mother – died, I didn't know what to do. I wanted to keep you, but I knew that it wasn't what was best for you. My dad was getting older and my mom was gone. I'm sorry, Will. I'm really sorry," he said sincerely. "I just did what I thought was best at the time."

The two sat statue-still, staring at each other. Will felt

crushed beneath the weight of his emotions. Larsen could see the sadness in his eyes. "I tried to find you, Will. But every time I got close the door got slammed in my face. Your adopted parents didn't want you to know me. They thought that was what was best for you, and I can't really blame them. It would have been hard on you," he huffed. "Maybe even harder than this." Larsen reached across the table, and just as he was about to embrace Will's hands, noticed the ring. His face flashed an expression somewhere between horror and joy. "Where did you get that?" he asked, pointing at it.

Will was confused by the look on Larsen's face. He had forgotten he was wearing it. "It's just a ring," he said innocently.

Larsen reached for it and excitedly slipped it off Will's finger. He recognized it immediately. His hands trembled as he studied it. He saw Sarah in it – the day he gave it to her, the expression on her face, their joy – all of it reflected in its modestly shimmering appearance.

"What's the matter..." Will began, but was interrupted before the question completely left his lips.

"Who gave this to you?" His voice was frantic, confused, demanding.

Will was baffled by Larsen's odd behavior. "Your father. Isaac gave it to me," he answered confused.

Larsen's face bleached white. He sat in awe, still studying the ring. Slowly lifting his head, he squeezed Will's eyes into his own and held them there. "My father's been dead for ten years. This is the ring I gave your mother the night I proposed to her." He paused, afraid to release his thoughts into words. "It was on her finger when she was buried."

Will lifted his hands to his forehead and shook his head. He couldn't bear to hear anymore. Larsen gently pulled his hands from his head. "Will. How did you get this ring?" he asked with calm composure.

He tried to speak, but couldn't.

"You've seen my father...Isaac. Where? How do you know it was him?" The questions came quickly and evenly.

The sound of Isaac's name gave Will courage. This time he found his voice. "I met your father, my grandfather, when I first moved here...in the cemetery. It was weird...he was always there...almost like he lived there. We talked. He gave me advice, told me stories. It was like he knew me." Will sensed Larsen's disbelief. He raised his voice. "His eyes...they were like ours," he blurted out convincingly. "He was tall and always wore a suit and some kind of old fashioned hat."

"His fedora," Larsen whispered.

"What?"

"His fedora. He always wore a fedora. He was buried in his favorite one."

Relieved that Larsen seemed to believe him, he lowered his voice. "When I saw him this morning he gave me the ring. He told me to be sure to give a message to the person it belonged to."

Larsen's deep blue eyes widened. "What did he say? What was the message?"

"He said that 'brick was the strongest foundation for a home.'"

The words suddenly took on their intended meaning for both of them. The dissonant sounds turned into a perfectly synchronized symphony as the last pieces of the puzzle slid perfectly into place. Isaac knew what his son wanted, and even more importantly, what Will needed.

CHAPTER 24

SUNSET

Will sat alone at the edge of the dock, solemnly staring out at the last of the sun's orange rays dancing on the lake. The quiet evening was broken with the occasional and sporadic calls of a lone bird readying for a restful night's sleep. His father and stepmother, "Angela" as he now called her, insisted that they all spend their honeymoon together at the spacious cottage they'd rented on the lake. Robert and Ian came too, the three boys inhabiting the furnished boathouse near the water. They spent their days swimming and jet skiing in the warm summer water, and their nights playing video games well into the morning hours.

A judge had decided that his adopted mother, Mrs. Karras, was an "unfit parent," and relinquished Will into Larsen's custody at his request. She rented a small one-bedroom apartment in Fairport, and successfully completed a 90-day drug and alcohol rehab program in Rochester. Her struggles and sobriety inspired her to enroll in fall classes at the community college. She wanted to earn her degree in drug counseling so she could help other people battle and beat their addictions. Will visited her every other weekend, and knew she would make it. He was proud of her.

Fortunately, he never had to face a judge about the assault complaint filed by the Bakers. Claiming that he had "had enough of that freakish Karras family," Dr. Baker dropped all charges. But most people knew it was because he didn't want to draw any more attention to the fact that a skinny and floppy-haired boy knocked out his Judo warrior son with one punch.

Like the lake he stared at, Will understood that things would change, the water calm one day, choppy another, frozen the next. But the real comfort came in knowing that, whatever form it took, the water would always be there for him. Now, for this very moment, it was as smooth as glass.

The light fading, he thought of his grandfather. It was Isaac's will, he knew, that brought him where he was today. Although he hadn't seen the wise old man since the cold winter's morning when he gave him his mother's ring, he knew that he would see him again in another sunset, in some other time, and in some other place.

THE END

Made in the USA
Lexington, KY
26 November 2009